Crime Fiction: A Very Short Introduction

VERY SHORT INTRODUCTIONS are for anyone wanting a stimulating and accessible way into a new subject. They are written by experts, and have been translated into more than 40 different languages.

The series began in 1995, and now covers a wide variety of topics in every discipline. The VSI library now contains over 350 volumes—a Very Short Introduction to everything from Psychology and Philosophy of Science to American History and Relativity—and continues to grow in every subject area.

Very Short Introductions available now:

ACCOUNTING Christopher Nobes
ADVERTISING Winston Fletcher
AFRICAN AMERICAN RELIGION
    Eddie S. Glaude Jr.
AFRICAN HISTORY John Parker and
    Richard Rathbone
AFRICAN RELIGIONS Jacob K. Olupona
AGNOSTICISM Robin Le Poidevin
ALEXANDER THE GREAT
    Hugh Bowden
AMERICAN HISTORY Paul S. Boyer
AMERICAN IMMIGRATION
    David A. Gerber
AMERICAN LEGAL HISTORY
    G. Edward White
AMERICAN POLITICAL HISTORY
    Donald Critchlow
AMERICAN POLITICAL PARTIES
    AND ELECTIONS L. Sandy Maisel
AMERICAN POLITICS
    Richard M. Valelly
THE AMERICAN PRESIDENCY
    Charles O. Jones
AMERICAN SLAVERY
    Heather Andrea Williams
THE AMERICAN WEST Stephen Aron
AMERICAN WOMEN'S HISTORY
    Susan Ware
ANAESTHESIA Aidan O'Donnell
ANARCHISM Colin Ward
ANCIENT ASSYRIA Karen Radner
ANCIENT EGYPT Ian Shaw
ANCIENT EGYPTIAN ART AND
    ARCHITECTURE Christina Riggs

ANCIENT GREECE Paul Cartledge
THE ANCIENT NEAR EAST
    Amanda H. Podany
ANCIENT PHILOSOPHY Julia Annas
ANCIENT WARFARE
    Harry Sidebottom
ANGELS David Albert Jones
ANGLICANISM Mark Chapman
THE ANGLO-SAXON AGE John Blair
THE ANIMAL KINGDOM
    Peter Holland
ANIMAL RIGHTS David DeGrazia
THE ANTARCTIC Klaus Dodds
ANTISEMITISM Steven Beller
ANXIETY Daniel Freeman and
    Jason Freeman
THE APOCRYPHAL GOSPELS
    Paul Foster
ARCHAEOLOGY Paul Bahn
ARCHITECTURE Andrew Ballantyne
ARISTOCRACY William Doyle
ARISTOTLE Jonathan Barnes
ART HISTORY Dana Arnold
ART THEORY Cynthia Freeland
ASTROBIOLOGY David C. Catling
ATHEISM Julian Baggini
AUGUSTINE Henry Chadwick
AUSTRALIA Kenneth Morgan
AUTISM Uta Frith
THE AVANT GARDE David Cottington
THE AZTECS David Carrasco
BACTERIA Sebastian G. B. Amyes
BARTHES Jonathan Culler
THE BEATS David Sterritt

Available soon:

For more information visit our website

www.oup.com/vsi

Richard Bradford

CRIME FICTION

A Very Short Introduction

OXFORD
UNIVERSITY PRESS

OXFORD
UNIVERSITY PRESS

Great Clarendon Street, Oxford, OX2 6DP,
United Kingdom

Oxford University Press is a department of the University of Oxford.
It furthers the University's objective of excellence in research, scholarship,
and education by publishing worldwide. Oxford is a registered trade mark of
Oxford University Press in the UK and in certain other countries

First edition published in 2015

Impression: 1

Published in the United States of America by Oxford University Press
198 Madison Avenue, New York, NY 10016, United States of America

British Library Cataloguing in Publication Data
Data available

Library of Congress Control Number: 2014957193

ISBN 978-0-19-965878-7

Printed in Great Britain by
Ashford Colour Press Ltd, Gosport, Hampshire

Links to third party websites are provided by Oxford in good faith and
for information only. Oxford disclaims any responsibility for the materials
contained in any third party website referenced in this work.

For Ames

Contents

Acknowledgements

Thanks are due to Emma Ma and Jenny Nugee of Oxford University Press for their help and patience, and to Tom Chandler for his excellent work as copyeditor. As usual, I am particularly grateful to Dr Amy Burns.

List of illustrations

Chapter 1
Origins

The 18th century and earlier

Crime has featured in literature for more than two millennia. In Sophocles' *Oedipus the King*, Oedipus might be regarded as precursor to the modern detective in that he conducts a meticulous investigation to unmask the murderer of his predecessor King Laius. Herodotus in *Rhampsinitus and the Masterthief* tells how the Egyptian ruler of the title attempts to capture a thief who is persistently stealing jewellery from the monarch's sealed vault. Another mythical larcenist, Cacus, features in the work of several writers, including Virgil; Cacus the cattle thief is brought to brutal and horrifying justice by Hercules whose herd he has recently raided. Susanna in the Old Testament Book of Daniel becomes the victim of a blackmail plot when two elders threaten to expose her, falsely, as an adulterer if she refuses to have sex with them; Daniel intervenes in the manner of a modern barrister, causing the two blackmailers to contradict each other; and justice is served.

More recently in *Hamlet*, Shakespeare's most celebrated play, every motive and act originates from Claudius' murder of Prince Hamlet's father; indeed until Act II Scene III when Claudius confesses while in prayer, his guilt is a matter for speculation, prompting comparisons with the mystery-driven narrative of modern crime fiction.

Outside Judeo-Christian culture stories such as Scheherazade's tale of 'The Three Apples', from *One Thousand and One Nights* include unresolved puzzles, in this specific case the discovery of the dismembered body of a young woman in a heavily locked chest in the river Tigris. Harun al-Rashid appoints a vizier—a junior minister or secretary—to investigate the killing and the story spirals into a sequence of pleas and confessions by figures who volunteer their accounts, following the vizier's failure to identify a culprit.

To treat these and similar narratives as prefigurings of the tradition that has thrived during the last two centuries is to blur and distort the definitive features of the latter. The Russian critic Tzvetan Todorov's essay 'The Typology of Detective Fiction' is regarded as the decisive account of how the genre works and of what differentiates it from other forms of novel writing. According to Todorov the classic crime novel is made up of two stories. Story one usually occurs before the narrative opens with a murder or some other criminal act, while story two involves characters who disclose aspects of story one to the reader, either through their methods of detection or via unwitting revelations. Todorov concedes that this formula is not comprehensive, noting that in the case of the thriller or what he calls the 'suspense' novel the reader might become aware of the identity of the perpetrator and the circumstances of the criminal act before these are known to the principal characters in story two. Nonetheless, he insists that in each instance we can locate a common feature: the tension between what is not known and the procedure by which the facts are exposed. In the classic detective novel the reader and the detective share the same perspectives and objective; to solve the crime and identify the perpetrator. Even though the detective might appear to outrank the reader in terms of their deductive and ratiocinative powers (an impression created by the author's command both of story one and the activities of the detective) we share his or her sense of story two as an intellectual challenge. In the thriller the alliance between the reader and the detective might be less secure, especially if we learn much of story one well before the conclusion of story two, but the factor that draws and sustains the reader's attention endures. We are excited by the prospect of uncertainty, of being uncertain of whether the crime will be solved.

In all of the works listed, from Sophocles through Scheherazade to *Hamlet*, a crime certainly occurs and often the narrative is compelled by its commission, but when we consider each of them in detail it is apparent that the unjust or arbitrarily cruel act is a thematic hinge for the exploration of more fundamental issues. Sophocles' Oedipus prefigures Prince Hamlet as an embodiment of psychological turmoil. Rhampsinitus' contest with the two brothers who steal his jewels is an, albeit gruesome, meditation on the nature of governance and fate, and Susanna's tale is a lesson in pre-Christian Judaic theology. The crimes or mysteries of these pieces are incidental and subordinate to other more significant themes and to read them in expectation of Todorov's notion of excitement-by-disclosure would be both perverse and ultimately frustrating.

Where, then, can be located the true origins of modern crime fiction? It began in England during the 18th century, or to be more accurate it is here that we can locate its miscellaneous sources. Daniel Defoe and Henry Fielding played significant parts in the founding of the novel in English and they had one more thing in common. Both had direct experience of criminality, the judicial system, and the punishments visited on those convicted. Defoe spent several years in jail and many of his early political pamphlets incorporate opinions on crime and judgement—while Fielding was a barrister and later a magistrate who also wrote widely on judicial practice and the maintenance of order and equanimity in society as a whole. Defoe's *Moll Flanders* (1722) is the story of the eponymous anti-heroine's life of crime and eventual repentance. Moll escapes the death penalty and faces, with Christian resignation, the lesser punishment of deportation to Virginia. In Fielding's

Joseph Andrews (1742) and *Tom Jones* (1749) prejudiced and ignorant squire magistrates feature regularly and are depicted by Fielding as a social contagion. The connection between all three works and crime novels of the late 19th century might seem tenuous—criminal misbehaviour and the dispensation of justice are presented naturalistically with no hint of mystery nor any invitation to participate in a process of detection—yet at the same time one detects in both authors an alertness to a prurient interest among readers in the often unedifying treatment of wrongdoers. Both men knew from experience that the judicial system and the stories attendant on major cases of arrest and trial amounted to the most popular form of entertainment of the period. Trials and public executions were often accompanied by hastily printed pamphlet-length biographies of the accused or narrative poems emphasizing the more thrilling and gruesome elements of their activities. Hundreds, often thousands, flocked to witness hangings and each event generated a supplement of lurid bestsellers. Eventually the state recognized the potentially degenerate nature of this and attempted to regulate popular tastes with the publication first, in 1728, of *Accounts of the lives, crimes, confessions and executions of criminals* ... all written by prison chaplains who extracted the necessary information from the prisoners, usually those sentenced to death, and their fellow inmates. These miniature biographies were frequently uneven in mood and purpose in that the life stories told by the condemned with an air of mischievous irresponsibility would then conclude with an incongruous note of contrition. One assumes that the latter was supplied by the chaplain irrespective of what the criminal actually felt about their past. One of these featured Mary Young, alias Jenny Diver, hanged in 1740. Her story of rising to become leader of a group of thieves reads like a piece of Rabelaisian fiction, causing us to doubt the authenticity of her repentant demeanour at the close of the tale. Although Defoe is far more accomplished at reconciling guilty exhilaration with moral probity one cannot help but notice parallels with *Moll Flanders*.

4

In 1773 the *Accounts* were replaced by the *Newgate Calendars* which presented a more reputable challenge to the privately printed pieces with their emphasis on the judiciary as an instrument for deterrence and maintenance of the moral values that criminals would eventually acknowledge, often shortly before their journey to the gallows. Nonetheless there endured throughout the 18th century a competitive relationship between the unofficial bestsellers, which paid rather spurious respect to morality while serving the baser instincts of popular taste—which were supplemented by a form of live mass entertainment that by far outranked the theatre in terms of its audience, with the actual execution of the principal figure—and the novel itself as a self-determined literary genre. Alongside such 'respectable' fictions as *Robinson Crusoe* (1719) and *Moll Flanders* (1722) Defoe produced two biographical accounts of the lives, careers, and eventual executions of Jack Sheppard the notorious house breaker (1724) and Jonathan Wild, gangster and informer who was responsible for Sheppard's arrest (1725). In 1743 Fielding produced a quasi-biography of Wild, in which the 'thief taker's' exploits invite comparisons with the activities of contemporary Whig politicians, and John Gay's immensely popular *The Beggar's Opera* (1728) involves a thinly disguised dramatization of the feud between Sheppard and Wild. During this period literature was transformed from a bohemian minority interest to a profitable industry and the newly emergent genre of fiction in particular was drawn instinctively towards subjects that attracted mass-market interest. Although the detective novel as we now understand it—the narrative that follows Todorov's model—would not emerge until the 19th century, there was during the nascent years of fiction itself an instinctive mutual attraction between the practice of putting stories into saleable printed form and a particular subject: crime.

Sheppard endured as a legendary anti-hero throughout the century and in 1839 he became, inadvertently, a transformative figure. Previously, in pieces by Defoe and Fielding, no attempt was made to alter the known facts of his life and fate. The early 19th century writer William Harrison Ainsworth reversed this relationship between fiction and fact and in *Jack Sheppard* (1839) presented the thief as an invention, which offered him far more licence than Defoe and Fielding to play upon the reader's prurient instincts. Fielding had energized an already exciting narrative yet was unable to change a foregone conclusion: his readers knew what would happen to Sheppard. But Ainsworth both exploited the largely undisputed truths of his subject's life while altering those parts of it he felt would further stimulate the reader's excitement, to the extent that we begin to wonder if in his version the outlaw might in some way avoid arrest and execution. Uncertainty overruled familiarity and throughout the richly dramatized account of the thief's exploits we are constantly engaged by the question of what will happen next—we feel that something is missing: who or what will succeed in bringing him to justice? Ainsworth's novel was effectively the fledgling detective novel. All it lacked was a detective and Ainsworth was not to blame for this. The novel was published only ten years after Sir Robert Peel founded the Metropolitan Police Force and in 1839 it was a somewhat shambolic institution, merely a slight improvement on the system of parish watchmen and constables it was designed to replace. A plainclothes division was not officially founded until 1869, though officers had sometimes worked undercover before that.

The book was the most popular and most controversial of the so-called 'Newgate' novels of the early 19th century. The subgenre's allusion to the prudent officially sanctioned accounts of crime, punishment, and remorse is misleading. Critics accused Ainsworth of glamorizing the outlaw and encouraging those among the lower orders able to read the book to follow his unwholesome example. Edward Bulwer Lytton's eponymous anti-hero *Paul Clifford* (1830) is, like Sheppard, a highwayman but Bulwer Lytton's story is a shameless case of a political allegory disguised as a thriller. Clifford elicits sympathy from the reader and becomes all the more effective as a vehicle for his author's polemic on the consequences of a corrupt governing gentry. William Godwin's *Caleb Williams*

(1794) and Dickens's *Oliver Twist* (1839) are also seen as carrying the hallmarks of the Newgate novel. Both consider the questions raised by the idea of criminality and society's response to it, and while Godwin is often treated as an early example of the psychological novella and Dickens as a precursor of morally robust Victorian classic realist fiction, both have something else in common. Like Ainsworth and Bulwer Lytton the procedure of determining guilt, even if the identity of the perpetrator is self-evident, is left largely to the reader. They are crime novels without detectives and, while the absence or reliability of such a character would be a feature of some of the more adventurous fiction in the 20th century, we routinely regard crime writing as a genre that was born with the introduction of a figure who, on the reader's behalf, exists in Todorov's story two while attempting to resolve the enigma of story one.

Poe and Collins

Following the period of the Newgate novels the history of crime writing is dominated by three authors, though which of them can claim to be the founder of its properly evolved form remains a matter for debate. Chronologically, Edgar Allan Poe (Figure 1) is the strongest candidate, with his invention of the crime-solving protagonist C. Auguste Dupin who appears in three short stories—'The Murders in the Rue Morgue' (1841), 'The Mystery of Marie Roget' (1842–3), and 'The Purloined Letter' (1844). Poe called these stories 'tales of ratiocination' and Dupin is certainly the first character in a novel about crime who makes use of his deductive skills to arrive at a solution to the transgressive act. In this sense he could be regarded as patriarch of a legacy that includes Holmes, Poirot, Miss Marple, Maigret, Father Brown, Sam Spade, John Rebus, et al. But while we might treat Poe as the founder of a tradition of problem-solving detectives we should also recognize that what appeared after him was very different from his idiosyncratic precedent.

1. Edgar Allan Poe. 'Edgar Allan Poe, who in his carelessly prodigal fashion, threw out the seeds from which so much of our present literature has sprung, was the father of the detective tale.' (Arthur Conan Doyle, 1901)

Almost as intriguing as the puzzle encountered and decoded by Dupin in 'The Murders in the Rue Morgue' is the mystery of why Poe composed such a story in the first place. The plot is legendary. Dupin, a well-educated Parisian with we assume a private income, and his unnamed companion who narrates the piece, take an interest in the recent murder of two women whose bodies are discovered in an apartment which is locked from the inside. By various means—including a cunning newspaper advertisement that entraps an unwitting accomplice—Dupin unravels the enigma that has confounded the local police, but we have to wonder if Poe intended to draw the reader into this macabre crossword puzzle that would become the keynote of mainstream crime fiction or whether his intention was rather more profound and high-minded. Dupin begins the tale with reflections on the problems of epistemology and reasoning, and one might be forgiven for regarding this as the preface to a fictionalized warning against the dangers of the Cartesian paradox rather than a detective mystery. And the puzzle, when solved, does nothing to dispel this suspicion. The 'murders' were committed by an orangutan, footloose from its owner and wielding a razor. It gains entry via a window that would be inaccessible to a human being and on departure accidentally allows the sash to descend, creating the impression that the apartment is, inexplicably, sealed. The scenario is preposterous and implausible, which again causes us to doubt that Poe was focused exclusively on launching a new subgenre of popular fiction. The ape—who is 'reprieved' by being sent to a zoo—drains the act of murder of its ghastly, tragic tenor. 'The Mystery of Marie Roget' is, conversely, based on an actual case, that of Mary Rogers whose body was found in the Hudson River in 1841. But once again the focal point is Dupin's intellectual acuity, this time involving what the investigator calls the 'Calculus of Probabilities' involving known facts on the habits, and the tendency to disappear, of women of the same class as Marie/Mary. The notional objective is to use broad statistical records to come to a conclusion regarding this particular murder and in this Dupin fails. Does Poe assume that his reader will be interested in attempting to solve a crime that by half way through the story is obviously beyond Dupin's, and everyone else's, powers of deduction? It is the equivalent of informing the reader of a conventional novel that the concluding chapter has been removed: satisfying, maybe, for fans of the avant-garde author B. S. Johnson, but hardly a reliable means of maintaining interest in the plot. Perhaps Poe is more concerned with the actual procedures of logic and reasoning when applied to urban degradation. In the 'Rue Morgue' story we find an anticipation of Rorschach psychology—only Dupin can discern two versions of events and pick out the one that everyone else overlooks—and in this one Dupin offers us a course in the practices and limitations of primitive sociology.

'The Purloined Letter' is almost as implausible as 'Rue Morgue', involving as it does the anonymous Minister D—who has stolen a letter from the Queen and is apparently using it to blackmail her. We never learn anything of Minister D—'s job, nor of where or what the Queen reigns over. At the time France had a monarchy, of sorts, but Poe ensures that parallels between his story and fact are vague. We remain equally uncertain about the content of the letter and, as a consequence, of whether a crime was intended or perpetrated. In this, the third of his Dupin tales, Poe continues to diminish the believable and the familiar at the expense of a very perverse meditation on our capacity to comprehend other human beings and their traits. So when Dupin is cited as the archetypal fictional detective we ought to consider the fact that the most vociferous debate on the significance of 'The Purloined Letter' was joined by mid-to-late 20th century literary theorists, notably Jacques Lacan, Jacques Derrida, Michel Foucault, and Barbara Johnson. None is concerned with its qualities, or otherwise, as a whodunit and it is difficult to suppress a smirk when imagining what fans of Christie or Chandler would make of, say, Lacan's wilfully incomprehensible 'seminar' on it. My point is that Poe's claim to being the originator of detective fiction is undermined by evidence that Dupin's role in the provision of solutions to crimes is incidental to his author's other somewhat idiosyncratic concerns. Before and after these three stories Poe published a considerable number of pieces in which mendacity, bizarre behaviour, and outright sadomasochism are the prevailing themes. For example, the primate–human trope emerges once more in 'Hop-Frog' (1849). In this case a court jester dresses the king and his ministers as apes and sets them on fire. No motive is adduced and no detective is present to disclose one. Similarly in 'The Black Cat' (1843) it is left to the reader to discern a logical or sane connection between the disfigurement of a cat and the (somehow less unsettling) axe-murder of a woman.

To return to the question: Was Dupin intended as the vehicle of a new branch of popular fiction or was he a subordinate feature of Poe's disquieting preoccupation with the grotesque? We should note that this was a period in which writers and publishers were desperate for new fashions which might excite the attention of a mass readership and that Dupin provoked no imitators. During the two decades following the publication of Poe's three stories the only significant development in crime fiction was the emergence of the so-called 'penny-dreadfuls', short novellas aimed at young urbanized working class men with a taste for the macabre. They were popularized versions of the Newgate novel, stylistically crude and concerned only with the graphic nature of usually violent criminal acts. Detectives hardly, if ever, featured in them and their seemingly unlicensed glorification of misconduct prompted the journalist and social commentator James Greenword to condemn them in 1874 as 'impure literature', 'contagious trash', and 'pen'orths of muck'. We must thus consider whether Dupin has been granted significance because we perceive him via the prism of Holmes and his numerous successors; at the time he left no discernible footprint on the literary landscape.

A respectable alternative to the penny-dreadfuls began to emerge at the end of the 1850s. The first quintessential 'Sensation' novel was Wilkie Collins's *The Woman in White* (1859) followed quickly by Mrs Henry Wood's *East Lynne* (1860–1), Mary Elizabeth Braddon's *Lady Audley's Secret* (1861–2), and Charles Reade's *Hard Cash* (1863). A common feature of their plots is that all characters are from an apparently decent, moneyed, upper-class background, which provides the ideal setting for narratives based on conspiracy, or fears of conspiracy, inheritances disputed or denied, and suspicions involving such secrets as bigamy and illegitimacy. During the early years of the genre no detectives featured in the novels. Certainly in *The Woman in White* Marian Halcombe and then Walter Hartright play an important part in unravelling the various subterfuges and deceits (crime in its crudest sense does not trouble them) and Robert Audley in *Lady Audley's Secret* reveals the eponymous aristocrat as a bigamist and attempted murderess. But in both instances the investigators are insiders, part of the same class, social circle, and often the same family as the perpetrators. It is almost as though the early Sensation novels were sending out a message to their bourgeois readers: we are a class above those who invite the scrutiny of policemen and we can deal with our own misdemeanours in a more dignified fashion.

A significant change occurred in 1868 with Collins's *The Moonstone*. T. S. Eliot called it 'the first, the longest, and the best of modern English detective novels' in 'a genre that was invented by Collins and not by Poe'; and Dorothy L Sayers and G. K. Chesterton agree that in their respective opinions it is the 'best' and the 'finest' detective story ever written. The stone of the title is a diamond brought to England from India by the odious Colonel Herncastle and inherited by his niece Rachel Verinder. Rachel wears it at her eighteenth birthday party and it is stolen later that same evening. There are four narrators: Gabriel Betteredge, the Verinders' head servant; Drusilla Clack, a disagreeable Evangelical Christian and Rachel's impoverished cousin; Mr Bruff, the family solicitor; and Ezra Jennings, assistant to the family physician Dr Candy, deformed, incurably ill, and addicted to opium. The fact that each of these observers is either slightly abnormal or by virtue of their social status marginal to the principal events causes us to discern the main characters and follow the narrative in ways that are variously partial and skewed. None can be relied upon as an entirely trustworthy witness for the simple reason that they know less about the events than those directly involved and this adds another layer of tension to the basic question of who stole the diamond.

It is the first Sensation novel to involve a police detective. Sergeant Cuff is based on the real-life Metropolitan police inspector Jonathan Whicher who had become a minor celebrity when he arrested Constance Kent on suspicion of murdering her 3-year-old step-brother. She was released without trial mainly because of the pressure of opinion, buttressed by the popular press, that the accusations of a working-class policeman, however convincing, should not take precedence over the plea of innocence by a young lady of proper breeding. Whether Collins was satirizing Whicher or criticizing the endemic snobbishness of mid-19th century England is a matter of opinion. Cuff is diligent and intelligent but he reaches the wrong conclusion. Instead the crime is solved by Franklin Blake, a gentleman adventurer who eventually marries Rachel.

Eliot does not substantiate his claim that Collins founded detective fiction but it is easy enough to postulate his rationale. Cuff is dealt with sympathetically but not without a hint of resigned condescension. The intellect, and by implication the breeding, of Blake triumphs and the gentleman amateur detective is born, as is the haughtily disconnected 'country-house' crime. Those who do not quite 'belong', by virtue of family or class, are consigned to the realms of puzzlement (and again this includes Cuff). Only those who share the same levels of discernment and discretion as the perpetrator of the crime are able to sift through the layers of false clues, suspects, and circumstantial red herrings to claim access to the truth. Crucially, the reader is caused to believe that they too belong within this circle of privilege.

Collins, brilliantly, invites us to treat the four narrators as inferiors (which Cuff fails to do), to read through their accounts, and join Rachel in her predicament and accompany Blake in his pursuit of a solution.

Arthur Conan Doyle

The Moonstone prefigured an enormous amount of later crime fiction but, like Poe's stories, it provoked no immediate imitations. As Julian Symons puts it, there was 'an interregnum' of roughly seventeen years between its publication and the appearance of the most famous of all fictional detectives. In Conan Doyle's *A Study in Scarlet* (1887) Holmes makes his claim to eminence by acknowledging the presence, and inferiority, of Poe's Dupin and the French novelist Gaboriau's Lecoq (see Chapter 4). The novel sold well enough but Holmes gained mass appeal when a series of short stories, collectively entitled *The Adventures of Sherlock Holmes*, appeared in *The Strand* between 1891 and 1894. Holmes's death in 'The Final Problem' (1894) turned out to be premature—because his followers had become addicted to him as something more than a literary creation. He had taken on the aura of a figure at once flawed and trustworthy, a very real presence whose apparent departure caused thousands to write to the *Strand*'s editor George Newnes pleading for his return. Doyle revived him in 1894 in *The Hound of the Baskervilles*, a novel serialized in *Strand*; its first instalment increased the already healthy sales figures of the magazine by 30,000. Overall Holmes—mostly but not exclusively with Dr Watson as his companion and narrator—featured in four novels and fifty-six short stories, the last of these going into print in 1927. All were set during the period from 1880 to 1914, with Holmes on one occasion acting on behalf of the British government against agents of the Kaiser at the beginning of World War I.

Why did Conan Doyle's creation earn the fascination, even adoration, of so many readers? In *A Study in Scarlet* Dr Watson seems fascinated by his friend's seemingly supernatural ability to solve crimes; fascinated because, at least by Watson's standards as a trained physician, he often seems a capricious dandy. During an aside for the reader he assesses Holmes's knowledge of literature, philosophy, astronomy, politics, botany, and geology on a scale from nil to twenty and finds that only occasionally does he rise above the former. His knowledge of chemistry is, perversely, 'profound' while as an anatomist he is 'accurate' but consistently 'unsystematic'. He has an 'immense' familiarity with 'Sensation' novels, plays the violin well, and is an exemplary boxer and swordsman. However, as the stories unfold Holmes gradually discloses a familiarity and competence in virtually all of those areas that in the first novel his friend judged him inadequate. Holmes is an enigma. He does not deliberately mislead Watson in their first case; rather Watson, despite his own considerable intelligence, can only appreciate the complexities of Holmes's personality and intellect in a gradual, incremental manner, as the stories and their friendship progress. This partly explains Conan Doyle's use of Watson as the lens for our perceptions of Holmes. Modern critics such as Knight (1980) and Shepherd (1985) often sound like Watson, finding fault with the suspect logic of Holmes's 'deductive' reasoning and treating the relationship between his pseudo-empirical methods—including the use of fingerprints, ballistics, and handwriting analysis—and the actual state of contemporary science as 'tenuous'. Even Julian Symons, admirer and fellow crime writer, has to concede that on a number of occasions Holmes is desperately flawed, such as in 'The Norwood Builder' when the 'charred organic remains', which turn out to be rabbit bones, persuade Holmes and Lestrade that Mr Jones Oldacre is dead. This, comments Symons, 'should surely not have deceived a Great Detective' (p. 86).

Most ascribe such blunders to Doyle, a consequence perhaps of his having to meet tight deadlines for *Strand*, particularly during those periods when writing supplemented his meagre income as a medical practitioner. But one cannot discount the possibility that Doyle deliberately causes us to notice Holmes's imperfections. The fact that he makes mistakes means that the reader is even more captivated by the paradox of a fallible investigator who never fails to solve the mystery. Doyle implies that Watson is a far better organized, more scrupulous figure than Holmes. In The Musgrave Ritual Watson describes, with patent dissatisfaction, the sheer chaos of 221b Baker Street, with papers and documents accumulating seemingly at random on every available surface, cigars kept in a coal scuttle, tobacco stuffed into the toe end of a Persian slipper, and months of unanswered correspondence gathering dust on the mantelpiece. And one can almost sense Watson shaking his head as he describes Holmes's recourse to chain smoking and often cocaine when tackling apparently unsolvable cases.

The result of this is that the late 19th century reader's affiliations were tantalizingly divided. Such readers belonged to the audience that Newnes discerned when he launched *Strand* magazine in the closing decade of the century: male, middle class, or with middle-class aspirations, who would purchase copies at railway station bookshops on their way home to the respectable and rapidly expanding suburbs of West London. For such individuals Doyle's stories avoided the garish melodrama of Sensation novels and the stench of lower-order prurience carried by penny-dreadfuls and their Newgate predecessors. They could be appreciated by the family patriarch but were thought suitable also for his wife and children. Watson was the steadying presence, the mirror image of the male middle-class reader, but he was also the gatekeeper to a world of fantasy. Holmes is a fabric of uncertainties. We are never quite sure about his background; his relationships with women are brief, tenuous, and largely beyond Watson's comprehension; and he operates as a morally astute alchemist, able to restore some sense of truth and justice to situations that confound both those involved and the police. For the reader on his train to the suburbs he offered escapist access to a cocaine-fuelled existence, unaccountable to authority, an employer, or family. He invites the reader to go with him from Todorov's story two to the secrets of story one, but once this reader leaves the train the focus shifts back towards Watson, Holmes's devoted but slightly disapproving acolyte.

Doyle should take credit for inventing the most charismatic of all amateur detectives but he also set a more significant precedent. The Holmes–Watson fictions enabled crime writing to appeal to an audience for whom the very notion of criminal misconduct was anathema: they were a class above the people who routinely committed such acts. At the same time the peculiar relationship between Holmes and Watson allowed them to experience the thrill of peeping at something dreadful in their neighbours' sitting room, while keeping their own curtains securely closed. This as we will see would be the keynote of the so-called 'Golden Age' of crime fiction.

The myth and legacy of Holmes is so robust and enduring that we sometimes assume that Doyle set out on his enterprise without competitors. In truth there were many, notably Arthur Morrison, Grant Allen, Matthias McDonnell Bodkin, and L. T. Meade, but the fact that they are largely unremembered reinforces the image of Holmes as a figure who left a unique imprint on all that would follow.

Morrison's detective, Martin Hewitt, is a modest everyman figure who treats the ordinary people of London, including its criminals, as his intellectual equals. Novels such as *Tales from Mean Streets* (1894) recall Dickens, without the humour, and look forward to Orwell. They disclose the levels of social exclusion and deprivation from which much urban crime originates and they did not appeal to the kind of reader who craved the seclusion of 221b Baker Street.

Allen treated crime writing as an unformed genre with considerable potential. He experimented with it as politico-economic satire, releasing criminals and detectives into the world of late 19th century capitalism as embodiments of its conflicting impulses of greed and order. *An African Millionaire* (1897) was well received by reviewers, sold modestly, and, in comparison with Doyle's work, plunged rapidly into obscurity.

L. T. Meade was the pen-name of Elizabeth Thomasina Meade who like Allen regarded crime fiction as an adjunct to more profound literary enterprises. Her particular interest was the nascent science of psychology and psychoanalysis which she saw as an explanation for all forms of criminal and socially deviant activity. She also regarded the age of machines and technology as potentially the cause of criminal madness. She contributed *Stories from the Sanctuary Club* (1899) to *Strand* but her readers were drawn to them as curiosities, a masochistic glimpse into what might occur in those parts of the expanding metropolis they would prefer to avoid.

Of all Conan Doyle's peers and competitors the most engaging is McDonnell, who creates a 'family' of detectives: Paul Beck, Dora Myrl, whom Beck eventually marries, and their son Paul junior. (See *The Capture of Paul Beck*, 1909.) The Becks seem to beg comparison with Holmes, emphasizing their reliance on capricious illogic as the best approach to the untangling of mysteries and the maintenance of justice. McDonnell's political career as a radical Irish Nationalist indicates, if only by implication, his opinion on Holmes's status. The Becks undermine his self-cultivated status as a bohemian outsider; by comparison he is a member of the English establishment.

Doyle was the writer who achieved a balance between the excitement of observing the crime and its solution and the security of doing so from a secure, morally aloof distance. More significantly, he became the test-case for crime fiction as a genre that might claim to be taken seriously. G. K. Chesterton's Father Brown stories (1913–35) are a rejoinder, part of a dialogue, with Doyle. Brown deals with evil and injustice according to the maxims of his Roman Catholic vocation, and the fact that Holmes had brought him into existence indicates that crime fiction had become a forum for the exchange on fundamental precepts of existence.

Chapter 2
The two ages: golden and hard-boiled

Agatha Christie

Most crime novelists of the Golden Age were British, notably
Agatha Christie, Marjorie Allingham, Anthony Berkeley, Dorothy
L. Sayers, and Michael Innes, though American writers such as
S. S. Van Dine, John Dickson Carr, and Ellery Queen followed
a similar template. Each of them produced their best-known
work during the three decades between the beginning of World
War I and the end of World War II (1914–45), and while there is
no clear consensus on why the period is referred to as 'Golden'
one can detect a certain cheerless irony among those who deal
with the term, especially from an early 21st century perspective.
Crime, at least in the hands of these novelists, is not so much
romanticized as dressed with a gloss of seemliness and propriety.
In this respect the Golden Ageists were scions of the Sensation
fraternity of half a century before, but while both are singularly
snobbish regarding the matter of where, how, and by whom the
deed is committed, the writers of the 1920s and 1930s seem
intent on securing the entire genre of crime fiction against any
accusations of realism or plausibility.

The term most frequently used to describe the quintessential
Golden Age crime novels is the plot-puzzle formula. Most detective

fiction surrenders the kind of narrative freedom available to conventional writers to a sequence of questions, mysteries, clues, and potential solutions that severely limit the activities of the principal characters and the trajectory of the story. A work in which the private detective spends the first two hundred pages in pursuit of a murderer and the closing seventy caring for his elderly parents without returning to the case would either be classified as a satirical comment on the genre or a postmodern revision of it. It would certainly not qualify as a traditional crime novel for the simple reason that when the detective, on instruction from his author, decides to give up on the puzzle and do something else he/she breaks the contract which defines both their role and genre. For the Golden Age writers, however, plot and puzzle were often so tightly intertwined as to leave no room whatsoever for the characters to display even a glint of independence. They frequently became automatons, servants to lifeless formulae.

The creations of Agatha Christie and Conan Doyle are the most prominent and enduring in all of crime fiction, both in terms of books sold and as adaptations in other media. Christie's Miss Marple and Hercule Poirot predominate as investigators and both are outsiders, in the most unthreatening and innocuous sense. Poirot is a Belgian expatriate practising his skills as amateur detective among the English middle classes and gentry. His nationality might be a backhanded compliment to Maigret but in other respects he seems to invite nothing but ridicule from those around him. He is short, plump, narcissistic, obsessed with domestic pettiness, and intellectually conceited. Miss Marple is ostentatiously English, the ageing spinster who has over-extended her stay in a novel by Jane Austen and now finds herself living from a modest annuity on the margins of communities in the introverted, snobbish, Home Counties during the years between the wars.

They might, potentially, have made use of a legacy pioneered by Doyle's Holmes and inherited by Chesterton's Father Brown, as figures who are by their own choice alienated from the worlds they investigate and are consequently granted a unique perspective on them. Instead Christie causes them to become intermediaries between the reader and the puzzle of the narrative. They are, like us, not quite part of the network of suspicions and deceptions that underpin the crime but at the same time they are our conduit to the tantalizing mystery of the novel.

In *The Murder at the Vicarage* (1930) the victim is Colonel Lucius Protheroe, resident of the otherwise tranquil village of St Mary Mead. Two different people confess to the crime and the scenario is further complicated by the fact that all other characters who feature in the novel, Protheroe's neighbours, admit to despising him. Even the vicar states that the locality would benefit from his departure. Few would regard the scenario as anything but ludicrous. Violent crimes were, sometimes, committed in prosperous parts of rural England but having the entire population of the village confronting an elderly spinster with uncorroborated alibis and resolute motives for murder was, as Christie and her readers knew, laughably improbable. Marple is, by virtue of her isolation and insularity, a proxy reader. A murder has been committed but Marple's preoccupation with the motives and movements of those potentially involved sanitizes it, cleanses it of its macabre and grotesque features. Instead it becomes a quiz, in which the characters become less like real people, variously guilt-ridden or distressed, than chess pieces, part of a game where we and Marple pit our skills against an anonymous adversary.

Christie's most famous work is *The Murder of Roger Ackroyd* (1926), set in the village of King's Abbott and narrated by Dr James Sheppard, who becomes the equivalent of Watson to Doyle's Holmes. The other characters introduce themselves as by part secretive, suspect, and involuntarily informative; each behaves entirely as we would expect them to in terms of their social rank and Miss Marple becomes the equivalent of the dealer in a card game, presiding over a tournament of chance, estimation, and guesswork.

The reviews of the novel were illuminating, with *The Scotsman* commenting that 'Everybody in the story appears to have a secret of his or her own hidden up the sleeve', and *The Observer*: 'No one is more adroit than Miss Christie in the manipulation of false clues and irrelevances and red herrings'. None of the reviewers finds that any of Christie's creations are endowed with prominent characteristics, endearing or otherwise. Certainly they behave according to rank and post (Major Blunt is the archetypal big game hunter, John Parker the dutifully routine butler) but beyond this they do not seem much possessed of a personality. Instead they are ciphers, embodiments of crossword-style clues.

Sayers and Allingham

Christie, to her credit, displays a degree of equanimity in the distribution of qualities such as discernment and intelligence, while never quite suggesting that the servants and lower orders are the equals of their social superiors; she did not wish to eclipse the game of deception with sociological observation. Dorothy L. Sayers, her contemporary, seems by comparison given to bouts of farce and caricature, or she might if her creations were not so ponderously unamusing. At first one begins to wonder if Sayers's detective, Lord Peter Wimsey, is designed to catch the more gullible among his fellow characters, and his readers, off-guard, cause them to assume that it will be easy to outwit such a buffoon, and then, from beneath the façade of a figure seemingly borrowed from P. G. Wodehouse, surprise them with a previously concealed razor-sharp intellect. But no, Wimsey is precisely what he appears to be, happy to complete expressions of enthusiasm or bafflement with 'what!' and constantly requesting his ever-reliable side-kick Bunter (Watson demoted to the rank of Wodehouse's Jeeves) to bring him such items as a bottle of 'rather decent' Château d'Yquem. Is Sayers suggesting that readers might join her in a side-long smirk at her creation? This seems unlikely given that her comments on him bustle with undisguised admiration. ('"Even I am baffled, but not for long!" he cried, with a magnificent burst of self-confidence.') The yokels who occasionally venture into the stories are, the two of them agree, almost subnormal and she seems happy to endorse Wimsey's casually racist and anti-Semitic comments on conspicuously non-English figures.

The Wimsey novels were as popular as those featuring Marple and Poirot, but before we condemn the reading public of the 1920s as lacking in anything resembling taste or discrimination we should remind ourselves that fans of Wimsey suspended any concern with realism or credibility. Indeed, characters and scenarios that were little other than fantastic were appropriate to what detective fiction had become. Sayers once had ambitions to be a poet and dramatist and had produced her first crime novel simply to avoid poverty. Later, in her introduction to *Great Short Stories of Detection, Mystery and Horror* (1928), she identifies the origins and status of the genre as non-literary, a variation on 'the pages of every magazine and newspaper [which] swarm with cross-words, mathematical tricks, puzzle pictures, enigmas, acrostics…'. It did not matter if her readers found Wimsey and his world preposterously unrealistic. They provided an environment closed-off from anything outside the novel and therefore ideally suited to the puzzle-plot that Golden Age detective fiction had become.

Wimsey might have been a gross exaggeration of the real-life aristocracy of the period but in the equally exclusive world of crime fiction he was one of many. His closest forerunner was probably H. C. Bailey's Mr Fortune (of *Call Mr Fortune*, 1920) who does not hold a title but displays the discerning, foolishly quixotic manner of one who should. Sir Henry Merrivale is a mere baronet but he enables Carter Dickson (a pseudonym of John Dickson Carr) to present murder as something that happens somewhere else, beyond the experiences of his readers. Margery Allingham's *Death of a Ghost* (1934) featured Albert Campion, lanky, bespectacled, eccentric and with family links to the upper reaches of the peerage, and, it is rumoured, the royal family. Even Ngaio Marsh, a New Zealander, cannot fully detach her professional detective Inspector (later Superintendent) Roderick Alleyn from associating with the nobility. His mother, we learn, is Lady Alleyn, breeder of Alsatians for discerning upper-class dog lovers.

The US Golden Age

The British obsession with socially elevated detectives found its most curious transatlantic manifestation in S. S. Van Dine's Philo Vance. Vance was a near contemporary of the creations of Chandler, Hammett, and Cain but he exists in a different universe. Vance is, in Van Dine's words, a 'young social aristocrat'. He has spent time at Oxford, professes a Nietzschean view of humanity as a whole, and before his return to America lived in a beautifully appointed residence just outside Florence. He is a ridiculously unreal creation and in this respect ideally suited to his role as quiz-master—if the reader took him seriously they might be distracted from the puzzle-plot of the novel.

In 1929 Father Ronald Knox, a US priest whose bishop eventually forbade him from writing crime fiction, published the 'Detective Story Decalogue', ten rules that every respectable crime writer must observe to ensure 'fair play'. Knox's tongue was planted firmly in cheek yet his list was accepted by most as an accurate account of the conventions that defined Golden Age writing in its heyday. It is a prescriptive anticipation of Todorov's two-story model, making it clear that clues must be distributed in the early to mid-sections of the novel ('The criminal must be mentioned in the early part of the story...'), but left for the detective, and the reader, to interpret. One of the most revealing of Knox's ordinances is the ninth: 'The stupid friend of the detective, the Watson, must not conceal any thoughts that pass through his mind...' There were certainly some variations on this formula but Knox catches well the dilemma faced by novelists who found themselves catering to readers more interested in an exercise in mental agility than a work of representation. Characters must conform to the roles allocated to them as functionaries in the puzzle and their personality must neither become too complex nor unpredictable to distract from this. For example, in Margery Allingham's *Flowers for the Judge* (1936) the victim is Paul Brande, one of three cousins who run the Barnabas publishing company. The chief suspect is Mike Wedgwood, another cousin who has been having a clandestine but unspecified relationship with Brande's wife Gina, an American. Gina is made up of stereotypical features; as an American she lends a degree of glamour to the otherwise staid atmosphere of early Edwardian London (the novel is set several decades before its publication), an environment personified by her soon-to-be-late husband, whom she clearly finds wearying. Mike, the youngest of the cousins, is more roguish and adventurous than the other members of the company and the family. So although no concrete evidence is disclosed until Campion begins his investigation into the position of the body, followed by the discovery of a rubber pipe that might have been attached to the exhaust of Mike's car, Campion, and the reader, have their suspicions aroused by ruthlessly foregrounded elements of Gina's and Mike's personalities. To Allingham's credit she endows each with a number of engaging and quixotic characteristics but as we encounter these we almost sense that she is struggling not to allow herself the same imaginative and representational range enjoyed by the literary novelist.

In the Ellery Queen volumes Queen features as both the investigator and the author, a unique experiment in first-person narrative. Never before had the principal character, the narrator, and the named author claimed to be the same person. Queen in his various manifestations was the creation of Frederic Dannay (real name, Daniel Nathan) and his cousin Manfred Lee (real name, Manford Lepofsky). He closely resembles Van Dine's Philo Vance but Dannay and Lee were beyond compare as purists of the puzzle-plot technique. They never disclosed how exactly they co-wrote their books but the distinction between characterization and setting and detailed cataloguing of clues was so stark as to lead their fellow crime novelist H. R. F. Keating to conclude that 'Fred Dannay [the logician]...produced the plots, the clues, and what would have to be deduced from them...and Manfred Lee clothed it all in words'. Typically a novel will open with a list of clues-as-attributes (the murderer is male; the murderer is left handed; the murderer smokes a pipe, etc.). Next the reader will be invited, along with Queen, to match these features against the characters assembled for scrutiny. Simultaneously, a list of probabilities, prominently motive and opportunity, will be presented. In the best-selling early novels, such as *The Dutch Shoe Mystery* (1931) and *The Greek Coffin Mystery* (1932), a page called 'Challenge to the Reader' appears around three-quarters of the way through. This takes the form of a statement to the reader that since all the clues needed to solve the case have now been presented, a solution can be reached from the substance of the narrative so far and that the remainder amounts to a challenge: can the reader reach the correct conclusion before Queen does so in the closing pages?

All of the factors that make up realist fiction—characterization, reported speech, situational and spatial context, etc.—are expediencies, subordinate to the intransigent force of clues and potential solutions.

The Queen novels were treated by some as the apex of Golden Age fiction (Allingham praised Dannay and Lee as contributing more to the crime genre than anyone else) and by others as its trough. Perhaps the two men should themselves be the most trusted commentators, because by the 1940s Queen has become a discordant feature in his own novels, which had gradually begun to reflect the tensions and uncertainties beneath the surface of American society. In *The Glass Village* (1954) the atmosphere of a small New England town crackles with the neuroses and obsessions of McCarthyism. A murder suspect is lynched and Queen does not appear in the novel.

The arrival of noir and hard-boiled

By 1954 the Golden Age had ended. Some of its more celebrated practitioners were still writing—Christie and Sayers included—and readers continued to treasure its anachronistic curiosities. Few, if any, had taken it seriously as anything more than a puzzle dressed in escapist prose but during its heyday its antithesis emerged in America. This new version of the subgenre was still crime writing but it could now begin to claim something from the legacies of the realist novel. In 1926 Joseph J. Shaw took over *Black Mask*, a 'pulp' magazine so called because its use of cheap recycled paper was thought by many an appropriate medium for lurid celebrations of violence. Pulps were the American equivalent of the 19th century British penny-dreadfuls with prurient thrills offered at the expense of style, characterization, and plot. Shaw, however, encouraged his writers to marry the spare idiomatic mode of Faulkner, Hemingway, and Steinbeck with a crime-based narrative.

The magazine's first significant serialization was Dashiell Hammett's *Red Harvest*, published as a single volume in 1929. Never before had documentary realism been combined with crime fiction in this way, with the unnamed narrator known only as the Continental Op and based on Hammett himself, who had worked for the Pinkerton Detective Agency. During his time with the Agency Hammett witnessed the miners' strike in Butte, Montana, which resulted in mine guards opening fire on pickets, injuring sixteen and killing one, Tom Manning. In *Red Harvest* he blurs one-to-one identification of the real individuals with their fictional counterparts while preserving the tenor of the events (the mine owners are presented as employing paramilitary brutality against the strikers). The novel often drifts towards tendentious social realism yet Hammett seems equally alert to a readership which relishes depictions of violence for their own sake; at one point Continental Op becomes involved in an entirely invented sequence of episodes where a woman is murdered by the leader of one of the factions, a gang war erupts between different groups of workers and he, the Op, is pursued as a suspect.

No one who read the book would fail to be gripped by its vivid depiction of how the Great Depression contributed to acts of corruption and oppression, but at the same time Hammett raises the question of whether the apolitical thrills of a crime mystery can be consolidated with the kind of novel that would within a decade win John Steinbeck the Pulitzer Prize (*The Grapes of Wrath*, 1939). The issue was complicated by the publication of, in the same year as Hammett's book, W. R. Burnett's *Little Caesar*, which tells the story of how Cesare Rico Bardello rose from his beginnings as an armed robber of liquor stores to become one of the most powerful mobsters in Chicago. Unlike Hammett, Burnett tries to avoid the glamorization of organized crime and the novel's dry, documentary manner also drains it of much that attracts readers to crime writing. We are never caused to wonder who is responsible for its events and the flat unemotional style of the narrator contrasts starkly with Continental Op's engagingly rough idiom.

The three most celebrated practitioners of what became known as the 'hard-boiled' or 'noir' brand of detective fiction were Hammett, James M. Cain, and Raymond Chandler. Hammett went on to write two of the best-known crime novels of the 20th century, *The Maltese Falcon* (1930) and *The Glass Key* (1931). Julian Symons compares *The Glass Key* with the best of Dickens's writing, claiming that it can 'stand comparison with any American novel of its decade' (p. 158), including works by Faulkner, and he was not referring here only to crime fiction. Hammett defers to the whodunit formulae of the late 19th century and the Golden Age but he does so with caustic resignation; he is, he implies, a writer who will connive at populism but carry into it more profound concerns. In Symons's view a 're-reading of [his best work] offers fresh revelations of the way in which a crime writer with sufficient skill and tact can use violent events to comment by indirection on life, art, society...' (p. 158).

Sam Spade of *The Maltese Falcon* has nothing in common with the amateur detectives of Conan Doyle and Christie. He involves himself in other people's messy and sometimes illegal activities only to make a living and he is himself a morally ambiguous figure. His world is one of deceit, greed, and sexual potency intercut by a narrative style that is cynical and ruthlessly sardonic. His successor in *The Glass Key*, Ned Beaumont, is a gambler and racketeer who becomes involved in detection by accident, through his friendship with, indeed devotion to, criminal politician Paul Madvig. Madvig persuades him to investigate the murder of a local senator's son. Thereafter the plot promises on several occasions to offer specific links between acts of violence, what motivates them, and their effects on all concerned, but at each point reneges on the offer. Madvig proves to be as ruthless as Beaumont always knew him to be yet we are never certain of what cements their friendship, nor do we really understand what drives Beaumont to continue to put at risk his health and life in pursuit of what seems to him and us, unresolvable solutions. The novel begs comparison with Dostoevsky's *Crime and Punishment* as a depiction of our more disturbing compulsions, yet at the same time Hammett's blend of wit and melancholy takes us in a different direction. It shows us a society that is unreformable, one that baits our worst ambitions; yet it robustly avoids moral judgement. The fact that these divergent elements are strung together by a single plot-line of transgressive criminality enables us to classify it as detective fiction, but at the same time causes us to wonder about the boundaries that separate this genre from the mainstream novel. One can, therefore, appreciate Symons's case in his praise for it.

James M. Cain's *The Postman Always Rings Twice* and his novella *Double Indemnity* (both 1934) were at the time controversial because of their emphasis upon sex as the primary motive for killing. In both, married women exploit the mutual attraction of haphazard encounters in order to persuade men to assist in the murder of their husbands. In *The Postman Always Rings Twice* Frank Chambers, a drifter, stops at a rural Californian diner and seems driven as much by hunger for the lips of Cora, the owner's wife, as the food: 'her lips stuck out in a way that made me want to mash them in for her'. When they do kiss, two days later, 'I bit her. I sunk my teeth into her lips so deep I could feel the blood spurt into my mouth. It was running down her neck when I carried her upstairs' (p. 9). This hors d'oeuvre of macabre eroticism is followed by a sequence of even more grotesque events, where Frank and Cora's efforts to kill her husband Nick suffer a form of foul natural justice when the pregnant Cora dies in a road accident as Frank tries to drive her to a hospital. The narrator is Frank, who tells the story while on death row hoping to complete his account before his execution. Cain's work has been regarded by some as gruesome melodrama but before we judge him so rashly we might take into account his reliance upon actual criminal cases. *Double Indemnity* was based on the widely publicized murder trial of Ruth Snyder and Judd Gray, both of whom were convicted and executed for the murder of Snyder's husband; they and their fictional counterparts hoped to claim an insurance policy. In life and in the novella the narrative tension was generated less by whodunit than whydunit, in that although monetary gain seems the obvious motive, newspaper readers were addicted to the case of Gray and Snyder because, thought Cain, each enabled them to indulge a form of sado-sexual fantasy. Cain, then a newspaper reporter, covered the 1927 trial. At first the novel appears to be a return of *The Postman Always Rings Twice*, albeit with a little more detail on the planning of the murder. Walter Huff is an insurance salesman and very cleverly Cain weaves together the tactical development of his and Phyllis's plan to fake her husband's suicide and the acceleration of their mutual attraction. He continually blurs any clear distinction of the likeliest motive—sex or monetary gain?—and this perfectly replicates the attraction of the trial for readers of the popular newspapers that ran daily reports of it. Snyder and Gray were not being tried for adultery but Cain the reporter senses that the combination of illicit sex and death—actual in terms of Snyder's husband, imminent for both of the accused if a guilty verdict was delivered—created for his readers a mixture of guilt, duplicity, and excitement that mirrored the events disclosed in the courtroom. The average, law-abiding reader could deceive themselves that they were witnessing the mechanisms of a fair and open system of justice while secretly re-enacting the impulses of the accused. Cain replicated this in the book, with Huff as the wry, disillusioned narrator, a man driven by his sexual and materialistic appetites yet able to perceive such instincts from a distance in a weary disinterested manner. However, as the narrative unfolds, so his certainty about where his acts might lead him unravels. He begins to suspect Phyllis of plotting against him and to lust after her stepdaughter Lola. Matters become even more complex when it seems possible that Phyllis has all along been conducting an affair with Lola's ex-boyfriend Nino Sachetti and that the two of them might be planning to murder him. Nothing as Byzantine as this was disclosed in the Gray and Snyder trial, but Huff's, and the reader's, increasing sense of fear and uncertainty can be treated at least as a refashioning of its various levels of prurience and surrogate excitement.

At its most primitive, Cain's work returns us to the appetites that fed demand for the *Newgate Calendar* and similar publications, yet in other respects it carries the imprint of literary fiction, particularly with the figure of Walter Huff. The narrative resembles a lengthy dramatic monologue, where his ostentatiously confident manner gradually fragments until we are left with a man no longer convinced of anything, including who he is.

Raymond Chandler

Chronologically, Raymond Chandler (Figure 2) was the last of the three major noir/hard-boiled writers to go into print. His first short story was accepted by *Black Mask* in 1933 and his debut novel, *The Big Sleep*, did not appear until 1939 when he was 51. He has, however, received far more esteem than any of his peers both from fellow crime writers and within the broader literary world. There are myriad reasons for this, not least the enduring respect earned by film adaptations of his work; but another factor is his

2. Raymond Chandler. 'The murder novel has always a depressing way of minding its own business, solving its own problems, and answering its own questions.' (Chandler, 1944)

authorship of a 1944 essay called 'The Simple Art of Murder', first published in *The Atlantic Monthly*. It was the first eloquent and intellectually challenging argument that crime fiction should be taken seriously. He treats Conan Doyle, Christie, Sayers, E. C. Bentley, and Allingham with something close to contempt, accusing them of producing 'light' fiction involving such quaint curiosities as 'hand wrought duelling pistols, curare and tropical fish'. On the Golden Age of crime fiction he comments that 'The English may not always be the best writers in the world but they are incomparably the best dull writers'. In Chandler's view Dashiell Hammett had opened a door on new vistas for the crime genre, an escape from its cloying middle-brow status towards a radicalism that holds up a mirror to a very imperfect world. In particular he praised Hammett's adoption of 'American language' as an unfiltered medium for realism and claimed that he 'gave murder back to the kind of people that commit it for reasons, not just to provide a corpse'. The phrase is rather chillingly ambiguous in that he seems to suggest that Hammett makes fictional murders more credible in terms of their circumstances and motives while at the same time allows for the possibility that Hammett might, commendably, be writing for the sort of people who are themselves capable of committing serious crimes. He adds that the world of such novels is 'a world in which gangsters can rule nations and almost rule cities…it is not a fragrant world, but it is a world you live'. However, before 'you', the reader, become content with or resigned to a zone of moral relativism, Chandler, in what must be the most frequently quoted passage on detective fiction, introduces a steadying presence:

> But down these mean streets a man must go who is not himself mean, who is neither tarnished nor afraid. The detective in this kind of story must be such a man. He is the hero; he is everything. He must be a complete man and a common man and yet an unusual man. He must be, to use a rather weathered phrase, a man of honor, by instinct, by inevitability, without thought of it, and certainly without saying it. He must be the best man in his world and a good enough man for any world. (pp. 991–2)

This character is magically intricate; comfortably attuned to the dreadful world, the 'mean streets' in which he plies his trade, yet, as a man of principle, a figure to be relied upon, indeed a hero, one who stands above it. In these few sentences Chandler at once distances himself from the comfortable hinterland of Golden Age fiction and compromises his own project. He is describing his most famous character, and narrator, Philip Marlowe. This is Marlowe in *The Big Sleep* describing General Winslow's greenhouse:

It opened on to a sort of vestibule that was about as warm as a slow oven. He came in after me, shut the outer door, opened an inner door and we went through that. Then it was really hot. The air was thick, wet, steamy and larded with the cloying smell of tropical orchids in bloom. The glass walls and roof were heavily misted and big drops of moisture splashed down on the plants. The light had an unreal, greenish color, like light filtered through an aquarium tank. The plants filled the place, a forest of them, with nasty, meaty leaves and stalks like the newly washed fingers of dead men. They smelled as overpowering as boiling alcohol under a blanket. (p. 592)

Aside from his private weaknesses and his skills as an investigator, Marlowe is evidently a lover of language. The smothering atmosphere of the greenhouse is less a warning to his safety than a prompt to his appetite for lush metaphor. One senses that as he cultivates the image of 'nasty, meaty leaves and stalks like the newly washed fingers of a dead man' he has ceased to be a private eye. Marlowe the writer has taken over, and later when he asks a blonde, after striking her with his gun, 'Did I hurt your head much?' and she replies, 'You and every other man I met' he is joined by Marlowe/Chandler the screenwriter. Chandler's world is a reflection of his witty, cynical manner and other figures in it become living testaments to his perfect ear for dialogue, irrespective of their role in the plot.

The differences between the first person accounts by Marlowe and the third person narratives in a number of Chandler's short stories are negligible. In his novels we are listening as much to Chandler as to his creations and as a consequence the foul scenarios and ruthless individuals we encounter are invested with something close to elegance. They very often retain their menace but we can't help but admire the skill and verve of the prose that contains them.

In Julian Symons's opinion 'There was a toughness in Hammett that Chandler lacked and did not appreciate. It comes through in his remark that Hammett could "say things he did not know how to say or feel the need of saying" but that "in his hands it had no

overtones, left no echo, evoked no image beyond a distant hill"'
(p. 163). In short Chandler damns himself with self-praise. He is,
as Symons agrees, a better writer than Hammett but because of
that a lesser crime writer.

Unless you have a specialized interest in this branch of crime
writing the trio of Chandler, Hammett, and Cain will be far better
known to you than figures such as Paul Cain (no relation),
Horace McCoy, or Cornell Woolrich. The reason for this, I would
contend, is that the former, led by Chandler, set new standards as
stylists. Again and again one will find them compared with
Hemingway, Steinbeck, and Faulkner as practitioners of a
medium by parts spare, unforgiving, and eloquent. By
implication, therefore, they aspired to meet criteria established
by 'literary' novelists. But is this the means by which we should
judge the quality of crime fiction, according to the standards of a
very different—and it is assumed, superior—genre? Woolrich's
The Bride Wore Black (1940) is a horrifying portrait of
miscarriages of justice; Paul Cain's *Fast One* (1933) offers a far
more lurid account of mob violence than Burnett's *Little Caesar*,
and McCoy's *They Shoot Horses Don't They?* (1935) was
celebrated by French critics as a rare American example of
existentialism, with a murder committed apparently without a
motive, except that the killer seems to exist in a society that has
abandoned respect for human beings. Each of these could claim
to be just as realistic as anything by Chandler, Cain, or Hammett,
in the sense that they treat crime as symptomatic of some
endemic failure in a collective will towards decency or fairness.
They are regarded as second rate for the simple reason that
they are stylistically undemonstrative, sometimes hurried and
inelegant. We will return to the question of how, if at all, crime
fiction should be evaluated in the closing chapter.

Chapter 3
Transitions

British reserve

Julian Symons's *Bloody Murder*, first published in 1972, ranks alongside Raymond Chandler's 'The Simple Art of Murder', which appeared twenty-eight years earlier, as a shrewd assessment of the state of their profession by crime fiction writers, though neither can be treated as entirely unbiased. Symons's overview is far more extensive than Chandler's, taking us back to the early 19th century and involving a detailed comparison between Britain and America. He finds that some things have changed, notably in the US where the Chandler generation have inspired a sequence of even more radical departures from the steady formulae of pre-1930s writing. He does not go quite so far as to accuse his fellow Britons of passionless torpor but one leaves his book with an impression of phlegmatic resignation: Britain, he suggests, has progressed little since the years of Christie. His assessment is reflected in his own writing. Symons is an accomplished stylist with an ear for the artless disclosures of dialogue that rivals the best American 'hard-boiled' novelists, but from his first book *A Man Called Jones* (1947) one detects a reluctance, perhaps an inability, to take his chosen genre seriously. Certainly in this and in several other pieces of the 1950s there is evidence that he wishes to distance himself from the mannerisms of the

Golden Age—Christie and Allingham were continuing to publish and sell during the fifties. Most of his early novels are based on police procedures conducted in the dull provinces of post-war Britain but these concessions to realism are always matched by an instinct to inject something like farce and caricature into the investigations of figures such as the appropriately named Inspector Bland, a man whose meticulous efficiency can bore suspects into paroxysms of confession. In the novels and in *Bloody Murder* he appears to have confronted and accepted an impasse: Britain, its police, and its criminals, are irretrievably dull and to write of them in any other way is a perversion of fact.

H. R. F. Keating, a near contemporary of Symons, seemed to have come to a similar conclusion when he located his early novels in post-independence Bombay where Inspector Ghote can operate beyond the routines and predictabilities of Britain.

Colin Watson began his career with *Coffin Scarcely Used* (1958) and his plodding Inspector Purbright bears a close resemblance to Symons's Bland. In 1971 Watson too produced a reflective survey of the state of British crime writing entitled *Snobbery with Violence*, which includes a dismissal of the Golden Age writers as class elitists who made use of improbable wrongdoings to reinforce their notion of an intellectual and moral hierarchy. He endorses instead a brand of realism involving policemen, probably of modest background, who have to deal with mundane acts of violence or theft in the English provinces. What he overlooks, understandably, is that having tried this, he and Symons had opted for an injection of self-caricature to preserve their work from unreadable drabness.

J. J. Marric (real name John Creasey) created Gideon, first Superintendent and later Commander, as a compromise between the remnants of the Golden Age and doomed attempts to portray dullness as anything other than dull. Gideon's position as senior CID officer at New Scotland Yard added a hint of glamour while allowing Marric to ground his stories in the convincing and the contemporary. The latter includes issues such as police corruption, domestic violence, drug trafficking (marijuana only, and the perpetrator is Chinese), and the effects on potential criminals of slum clearance; not the sort of transgressions likely to concern Poirot or his fellow Orient-Express journeyers. Nonetheless, Gideon is in some ways a throwback to the pre-war mode. He is a resolute, honourable family man whose faith in the probity of the system he serves is unswerving, a bourgeois, officer-class forerunner of Dixon of Dock Green.

A few years after the Gideon series of novels came to an end at the close of the 1950s another English writer considered how he might make a mid-20th century senior police detective both credible and challenging. Nicholas Freeling decided that London, let alone the British provinces, was an unwelcoming location for such a project and like Keating he sent a very Anglocentric policeman abroad. Freeling's Van der Valk works in Amsterdam from which many, little more than sixteen years earlier, had been deported to the Nazi death camps. Memories of the war and Holland's liberal consensus of the early 1960s made Van der Valk's city a far more electric environment than anything that could be found in Britain.

From the mid-1960s to the early 21st century the mainstays of British detective fiction have been Reginald Hill, Colin Dexter, Ruth Rendell (aka Barbara Vine), R. D. Wingfield, Ian Rankin, and P. D. James. All have regularly produced bestsellers and their creations have become embedded in our cultural infrastructure via television adaptations. They have two particular features in common: a tendency to reinforce the legal ordinances and moral codes that are supposed to maintain order in our society and a preoccupation with class that endures as the legacy of Christie, Allingham, et al.

Dexter's Morse, the Detective Inspector without a Christian name, operates as an intermediary between the enclosed micro-societies of Oxford colleges—he is himself a graduate of the university—and the apparent vulgarity of the world outside. Certainly dons and students are just as capable of vile malevolent acts as their non-academic counterparts and, while Dexter makes no excuse for them, they embody a sense of ascetic exclusivity that causes their crimes to appear a little more polite and discriminating than most. There are echoes of the Country House mystery here and Morse's junior Sergeant Lewis, with his doses of working-class common sense, reminds us of the decent yet subservient lower-order characters in the works of Collins and Doyle.

This formula is reversed yet kept intact with Hill's Detective Superintendent Dalziel, a corpulent Yorkshire hedonist with an inclination towards brutality when conventional methods of detection fail him. He is preserved from moral dereliction by the continuous presence of Pascoe, a *Guardian*-reading, politically correct graduate. They operate like Inspector Jekyll and Superintendent Hyde, but their roles are not quite equal: we know that while Dalziel provides the drive and entertainment he would ruin himself and others without his educated middle-class anchor man. Rendell's Inspector Wexford is a mid-cultural approximation of Morse and more comfortably suburban than Dalziel, and Sergeant Burden is his unostentatious intellectual equal. Both are clever in an artless manner—unlike Morse they do not exhibit their particular preferences in opera or philosophy—and most significantly they know their place and respect the status of others: they are second-generation Gideons.

P. D. James's Commander Dalgleish first appeared in 1962 in her debut novel *Cover her Face*. He has endured for more than fifty years and must by now, at least in real time, be in his eighties, though in other respects he seems to have avoided any significant signs of ageing. In 1999 James reflected on her career, stating that 'It didn't occur to me either to begin with anything other than a detective story. They had formed my own recreational reading in adolescence...' She adds that Sayers and

Allingham had influenced her but that while the 'construction of a detective story may be formulaic; the writing need not be'. She implies that there are opportunities for a good writer to aspire beyond the 'recreational' status of crime writing without entirely abandoning its traditional formulae and this is what she attempts to do with Dalgleish. He maintains an enigmatic aloofness from the more base and vulgar tendencies of England in the late 20th century; he is a published poet, a dimension of his life that seems, intentionally or not, an antidote to the abominations of violence and death that he encounters in every novel. Morse, the senior detective and aesthete, is improbable but Dalgleish takes this mismatching of roles and traits a stage further and he ought to appear as a modern version of Holmes, distractedly brilliant, otherworldly, and entirely unsuited to the management-style routines of police work. Yet he does not. He could have walked out of a novel by Iris Murdoch or Aldous Huxley; disenchanted and unselfish, unable to explain the things he apprehends but alert to ideals that can, just, prove impermeable to degeneration. He should not belong in a crime novel but it is a testament to James's skill as a writer that we find him suitable to such a setting.

Until the 1990s when, as we shall see, a few changes were noteworthy, British crime fiction tied itself to self-limiting conventions similar to those that inform the medieval morality play or the kind of Victorian novel which promulgated the ethical norms of the period. Characters and circumstances are made believable only to the extent that they do not fail in their predetermined functions as indices either to abstract codes of behaviour or to idealized perceptions of the police, the judiciary, and society. Marric's Gideon acknowledges the possibility of police corruption, Dalziel exhibits numerous moral imperfections, and Rebus wrestles with his drink problem as well as, implicitly, favouring the rough end of Edinburgh society, the home of its professional criminals, above its middle classes. Throughout, these matters are represented as uncommon aberrations or indications that policemen are, more often than not, scions of the uncouth proletariat presently serving the greater public good.

US radicalism

During the same period American crime fiction showed itself more inclined to transgress such precepts, often by shifting the narrative focus away from the mindset of the investigator and toward the perpetrator, a procedure which carries an attendant question: might you, reader, be capable of this? James M. Cain allowed for this disturbing permutation on recreational reading, but Patricia Highsmith took it a stage further. Her first novel *Strangers On A Train* (1949) was immortalized by Hitchcock's film adaptation. The opening scenario is believable and mildly amusing: an architect of modest background meets a wealthy, garrulous socialite in a first-class train compartment. When the latter suggests a solution to their respective problems—one apparently motiveless murder in exchange for another—it seems like a grotesque, drink-fuelled conversation and nothing more. At least until the first murder is committed and the morality and consequences of killing cease to become matters of choice.

Her *The Talented Mr. Ripley* (1955) distorts and overturns every convention of crime fiction writing. Tom Ripley is asked by the wealthy shipping magnate Herbert Greenleaf to go to Europe and persuade his son Dickie to exchange his bohemian sojourn in Italy for the family business in the US. From the start Ripley's world is based on fraudulence and evasion—Greenleaf only asks him to 'rescue' his son because he believes they were fellow undergraduates at Princeton, but Ripley has lied about this—and on his arrival in Italy deception blends with fantasy and envy. Not only does Ripley succeed in persuading Dickie that they have met before, he gradually develops an erotic obsession with his world. Eventually he kills Dickie but proves far more ingenious than the Italian policemen. He escapes arrest through four further novels, pursuing a regime of apparently gratuitous killings while sating his appetite for high culture and philosophy.

It could of course be argued that Ripley is as unreal as figures such as Holmes or Miss Marple, yet it cannot be denied that Highsmith is far more ruthless and effective than any of her predecessors in causing the reader to confront murder as something other than a literary device or the trigger for a puzzle: we might not have met anyone like Ripley but when he kills people we cannot release ourselves from his horrifyingly real presence.

While Ripley continued with his expatriate homicidal activities in Europe crime fiction in America began on a trajectory that would eventually decouple it completely from its British counterpart. John Ball's *In the Heat of the Night* (1965) is remembered better for its 1967 film adaptation starring Rod Steiger and Sidney Poitier than as a novel, and the film, brilliant in its own right, did not significantly alter Ball's text. Ball found that mid-1960s USA provided one of the few opportunities for detective writing to become, unapologetically and without distraction, serious literature. Virgil Tibbs, a meticulous and efficient police detective from the liberal north, is caught between trains in small-town Mississippi where a racist segregationist mindset has obtained since the Civil War. Tibbs is arrested for a murder because he is an outsider, unable to prove his explanation for being in the railway station, and most significantly because his assumed guilt is predetermined for another reason: he is black. When Tibbs is disclosed to be a police officer he is co-opted as detective and absolved of suspicion but it is a partial, incomplete transformation: he is treated with grudging acceptance by the Sheriff's officers and with distaste and contempt by everyone else, including those suspected of committing the murder.

When Ball wrote the novel Civil Rights campaigners from the north were drawing national and international attention to a state of apartheid that endured in much of the American south. Tibbs was the instrument for a genuinely thrilling detective novel which follows the classic Todorov formula of two stories. At the same time his experience epitomized a clash of ideologies between an America that wished to institute progressive laws and mores and one that was anchored in 19th century prejudices.

In 1970 George V. Higgins launched his career with *The Friends of Eddie Coyle*, the like of which had never been produced before. Coyle is a low-level gunrunner for the Boston-based criminal fraternity and offered an alternative to prison by Federal Agent Dave Foley who persuades him to continue to work with a gang, now committing regular bank robberies, and inform on them. There follows a swirling narrative of deceptions, clumsy arrests—one involving the death of a suspect—and mismanaged assassination attempts. Higgins had previously worked as a lawyer and an Assistant District Attorney. He knew the world of police practice and criminal activity intimately and he had long before lost faith in any ideals as to who held the moral high ground. The novel is an example of documentary realism at its most cheerless. Higgins almost dispenses with a narrator, making use only of short phrases to choreograph a story made up largely of reported speech in its most undiluted idiomatic form, and this in turn provides him with an ideal format for the novel's bleak abstention from commentary or judgement. We watch as each character, on each side of the judicial divide, behaves with varying degrees of desperation, vindictiveness, and expediency but we find it impossible to identify a moral exemplar or an emotional affiliate. We simply observe, perhaps with horror or disinterest, depending on our disposition. In the end Coyle is murdered by a contract killer assigned to dispatch him by a senior mobster, and all that registers is our sense of the grim irony embedded in the word 'Friends' in the title of the book. Coyle has no friends, certainly not Agent Foley, who ultimately is as responsible for his death as the man who pulls the trigger.

The most unorthodox American crime novel of the post-war years is Ira Levin's *A Kiss Before Dying* (1953), the story of Bud Corliss who returns from wartime service in the Pacific and succeeds in murdering two of the three Kingship sisters, scions of a wealthy industrial dynasty. The book's gritty realism reminds one of Steinbeck or Hemingway, but this is shot through with a macabre mood that is at once addictive and repulsive. We are compelled to read on to see what Corliss will do next but we feel guilty about this. His primary intention is to marry one of the sisters and enjoy his share of their vast inheritance but through various unforeseen moments of incaution and paranoia—including a pregnancy—he finds himself obliged to kill each of them in order to pursue the next. We ought to detect in Corliss something close to madness or evil but Levin shows us only the kind of ruthless ambition that we ourselves might feel, and poses the question: might *we* be capable of acting like him?

Ball, Highsmith, and Higgins are extraordinarily different writers both in terms of technique and subject matter yet at the same time they share a significant common factor. Each goes much further than any of their British counterparts in their attempt to turn crime fiction into a genre that challenges our notions of violence, the law, and the social fabric that claims to account for both. Among the 'hard-boiled' writers there had been signs since the 1940s that Chandler's man of courage and 'honour' was being edged aside by less scrupulous figures, notably Mickey Spillane's Mike Hammer who made his debut in *I, the Jury* in 1947 and continued for the next four decades to wreak havoc among the criminal classes and the agencies of order and justice. The title of this novel represents clearly enough Hammer's credo and his attraction for a certain kind of reader. He is a vigilante, happy to dispense proper justice—usually death—when the mechanisms of police procedure and the judiciary might allow truly unpleasant figures to continue with their practices or, if apprehended, avoid an appropriate punishment. Spillane's work taps into the disquieting appetite for voyeurism that popularized the Newgate publications, except that his readers' fantasies were not fed by highwaymen anti-heroes. Rather, Mike Hammer incited the lynch-mob sentiment that proper retribution should be inflicted when the state proves too weak or ineffectual.

Spillane's Hammer is at once ruthless and melodramatic. He does terrible things, and we should gasp, but we cannot take him seriously. When, at the end of *I, the Jury*, Hammer shoots the beautiful psychiatrist (and murderess) in the stomach and she asks 'How could you?' (she has made several attempts to get him into bed), he answers: 'It was easy.' There was always a narrow line between the tough realism of figures created by Hammett, Cain, and Chandler and their exclusively machismo escapism. Spillane abandons all concessions to the former, but 1971 saw the appearance of a novel which completely undermined the presumption that crime writing would by its nature never be capable of reflecting the world we live in.

Joseph Wambaugh wrote *The New Centurions* (1971) when he was an officer in the Los Angeles Police Department. He was directly involved in the 1965 Watts Riots which feature at the end of the book and he distributes his experiences and observations as a policeman among the three principal protagonists, Serge Duran, Gus Plebesly, and Roy Fehler. They were classmates at the police academy and thereafter their professional and private lives only occasionally intersect, but they offer perspectives on the routines and pressures of police work never before found in a work of fiction. Wambaugh moves us as far as is possible from the whodunit formula of the genre without entirely dispensing with a claim to being a crime writer. The brutal actuality of murder and rape are frankly rendered and we are less concerned with the puzzle of who committed these acts than with their horrible nature. Most significantly, Wambaugh shifts the focus away from the policeman as the shrewd detective to the effects that working in such an environment have on his trio of characters, all of whom seem at various points driven in desperation towards adultery, attempted suicide, alcoholism, and racism.

In *The Choirboys* (1975) he is far less restrained. The Choirboys are a group of ten dissolute officers from the Wilshire Division of the LA Police Department who hold 'practices' in MacArthur Park involving violence, plots against their loathed superiors, and regular group sex with two barmaids of the locality. Sometimes the anarchic plot veers towards black comedy but just as frequently we catch glimpses of how each of them has ruined both their own lives and those of their friends and families because of their jobs. Even Henry 'Roscoe' Rules—violent bully, racist, misanthrope, and misogynist—is clearly more a driven man than an intrinsically evil one.

Elmore Leonard began his literary career writing Westerns and first attempted crime fiction with *The Big Bounce* (1969). His work combines Wambaugh's amoral naturalism with the louche somewhat distracted heroism of Chandler's most memorable figures. In *Pronto* (1993) for example, 66-year-old Miami bookmaker Harry Arno plans to retire, to Rapallo, a resort he recalls from his army service. It seems to him both legendary and magical: when there he talked with the incarcerated Ezra Pound. His retirement fund is made up of a million dollars he has systematically 'skimmed' from the mob boss Jimmy 'Cap' Capotorto. Eventually various gangsters, hit men, and a US Marshal are drawn into Harry's self-constructed picaresque plot. We know that he is a criminal but our interest is buoyed not, as in the traditional crime novel, by the question of who committed the crime or even of whether they will be brought to justice. Instead we desperately want him to escape the clutches of the mob and the law and live on his ill-gotten gains in a villa on the coast of Italy.

Frequently Leonard plays games with our sense of moral equivalence: some characters are reprehensible but they are quite likely to show themselves, by nature or deed, to be an improvement on the truly vile individuals from the same grey areas of criminality and misbehaviour. Officers of the law, in the meantime, are necessary restraints to anarchy but not people we are invited to wholeheartedly admire. Leonard's finest achievement is as a stylist. His third person mode evokes a companionship of uncertainty where nothing is clearly good or bad. *Killshot* (1989) opens with 'Blackbird' Degas contemplating his drink problem:

> The Blackbird told himself he was drinking too much because he lived in this hotel and the Silver Dollar was close by, right downstairs. Try to walk out the door past it. Try to come along Spadina Avenue, see that goddamn Silver Dollar sign, hundreds of light bulbs in your face, and not be drawn in there. Have a few drinks before coming up to this room with a ceiling that looked like a road map, all the cracks in it.

In *City Primeval* (1980) Raymond Cruz meditates on his appearance:

> He could be dry-serious like Norbert Bryl, he could be dry-cool like Wendell Robinson, he could be crude and a little crazy like Jerry Hunter...or he could appear quietly unaffected, stand with hands in the pockets of his dark suit, expression solemn beneath the gunfighter moustache...and the girl from the *News* would see it as his Dodge City pose: the daguerreotype police officer.

Degas is a psychotic hitman and Cruz a police officer. Leonard does not pretend that the former is anything other than evil and the latter as good as he can be, but their co-presence in the seductive stylistic mélange blurs any clear perception of their relative moral standing.

Wambaugh and James Ellroy established a basic precedent for the more adventurous American crime writers of the post-1960s decades.

Walter Mosley's black private investigator Easy Rawlins acts as a lens for the strata of exploitative violence, corruption, and racism in US society from the 1940s to the 1960s (though the novels in which he features began to appear in 1990 with *Devil in a Blue Dress*). He is a decent man but no better than he has to be, distrusting the police and the legal system as a whole and often surviving via his ability to incite fear in others. Mosley's exercises in dispassionate naturalism find a more disturbing echo in Lawrence Black's Keller (*Hit List*, 2000). Keller occupies the centre of the narrative as a compelling, beguiling presence, a man of dry wit and integrity. His profession? Self-employed hit man. James Ellroy in *American Tabloid* (1995), *White Jazz* (1992), and *The Cold Six Thousand* (2001) intercuts invention with meticulously researched scenarios from US politics and social history of the 1950s and 1960s. J. F. and Edward Kennedy appear alongside, and sometimes meet, figures from the Mafia and characters—some fictional, some actual—who frequently cross the line between CIA-sponsored terrorism and pure criminality.

Transatlantic contrasts

The British writer best known to have made rather modest claims upon the US form of unbridled crime fiction is Ian Rankin, whose series involving the Edinburgh-based Inspector John Rebus began with *Knots and Crosses* (1987). Rebus is prone to depressive bouts of introspection, often accompanied by infusions of alcohol, and he seems by temperament and background to fit in with the rough urban working classes who are responsible for much of Edinburgh's day-to-day fabric of criminality. At the same time, however, he never quite dishonours his profession; his litany of failed relationships is presented as a tragic consequence of his commitment to the job, and he views, and has the reader view, with circumspect disdain the pomposities of the Edinburgh middle classes and nouveaux riches. Some have treated Rebus's fictional environment as comparable with that created by Irvine Welsh but this is part of the questionable mythology of the Scottish literary renaissance. In truth, Rebus is only a little more unorthodox than the likes of Dalziel and R. D. Wingfield's Frost. He makes something of his existential crises and coat-trails his working-class Scottishness, with its collision of roughness and vulnerability, but beyond that the formulae that inhibit the mainstream of British crime fiction remain undisturbed.

By far the most impressive British crime writer of the 1970s–1990s period is Bill James. Sadly and unconscionably he is also the least recognized, featuring neither in *The Cambridge Companion to Crime Fiction*, nor the *Blackwell Companion to Crime Fiction*. James's novels, involving principally, though not exclusively, Detective Chief Superintendent Colin Harpur and Assistant Chief Constable Desmond Iles, have run from *You'd Better Believe It* (1985) to *Undercover* (2012) and the moral and ethical truancies of his policemen bring to mind Wambaugh and Ellroy. Harpur is a serial adulterer who is particularly besotted with Denise, a local undergraduate student almost half his age. His wife, Megan, begins an affair with an ex-colleague, recently promoted to the Metropolitan Police, and, in *Roses, Roses* (1993), is stabbed to death—probably by the henchman of a villain Harpur has had sent down, we never know—during her return from London. Iles, a man of lupine sophistication and dry wit, spends some of his time berating the liberal imbecilities of his senior, Lane, while occasionally exploding into almost murderous spasms of rage against both colleagues and villains, particularly those among the former, Harpur included, who have slept with his wife.

Iles attempts, habitually, to seduce one of Harpur's teenage daughters and for downmarket lechery trawls the docks for as yet un-fallen virgins whom he can rescue from local pimps, but always ensuring that he has sex with them first. Also, he murders a local gangster, who seems immune from prosecution, in a particularly sadistic, ritualistic manner. Add to this cast Jack Lamb, a wealthy dealer in stolen art protected by Harpur as his best informer, plus 'Panicking' Ralph Ember, sex addict, killer, and keeper of the bar where most of the local criminal desolates gather, and you have a menu that is a bizarre throwback to William Harrison Ainsworth's *Jack Sheppard. A Romance* (1839).

Alongside his fascinatingly grotesque cast James is a consummate stylist, bringing to the rather staid mechanisms of the crime novel a learned darkly comic bitterness redolent of Waugh or the Amises, father and son.

The only UK author who can rival James for unorthodoxy is Jake Arnott. *The Long Firm* (1999) was celebrated as the most original crime novel in living memory but in truth it is an adaptation of the techniques of James Ellroy to a British setting, specifically London in the mid-1960s. Like Ellroy, Arnott furnishes the text with enough period detail to secure authenticity without clogging the narrative, and more significantly he interweaves invented characters and events with some very real ones. The Krays, Tom Driberg, Peter Rachman, Evelyn Waugh, Liza Minnelli, and Johnnie Ray all play cameo roles which both correspond with biographical fact and often cross the line into the realm of the possible and credible. Ruby, Rachman's sometime lover, informs us that he prefers sex on top and facing away from her and Lord 'Teddy' Thursby notes in his diary that at the previous night's party he 'Nearly tripped over Tom Driberg, Honourable Member for Barking, on his knees, energetically sucking away'.

Arnott's overall objective, one suspects, is to impart to crime fiction a degree of purpose and gravitas, to shift it beyond its popular status as an easy recreational mode to that which engages the reader at a deeper intellectual and temperamental level. His choice of the 1960s testifies to this in that it is routinely regarded as the decade in which Britain finally unshackled itself from the codes of morality and behaviour and the class-based social structure that had been its formative elements for the previous century. Arnott addresses many of these issues, most specifically sexuality: he presents Harry Starks as openly, energetically homosexual, while in all other respects the complete antithesis of the stereotypical figures that were and still are associated with gayness. Significant political events such as the abolition of the death penalty and the legalization of homosexual acts are sewn into the chronology and it is evident that Arnott is, in part, offering an alternative account of the recent history of British society, obliging us to look behind official mythology to a world in which policemen and politicians are habitually corrupt and certainly not morally superior to professional criminals. It was clearly influenced by Ellroy's *American Tabloid* (1995) in which Peter Bondurant, Howard Hughes's confidant and fixer, Jimmy Hoffa's hit man, and occasional CIA operative, and Kemper Boyd, favourite of FBI boss Hoover, offer us a tour through the hidden, violent, often deranged world of American politics and law enforcement. Ellroy extended his state-of-the-deplorable-nation exercise into *The Cold Six Thousand* (2001), involving new characters and mature versions of the originals, as does Arnott in *He Kills Coppers* (2001). In this he introduces the adhesive tabloid journalist Tony Meehan who witnesses the abundant foulness beneath the tacky spectacle of England from the 1966 World Cup victory to the Thatcher years, and in *Truecrime* (2003) we reach the 1990s accompanied by some of the phlegmatic ageing figures from *The Long Firm*, Harry and Ruby included.

Several other British writers have tilted at precedent, but compared with James and Arnott their gestures seem innocuous. Sarah Dunant's Hannah Wolfe is the first British postfeminist private detective (*Birthmarks*, 1991; *Fatlands*, 1993, and *Under My Skin*, 1995), Judith Cutler's D. S. Kate Power is her CID counterpart (*Power Games*, 2000), and Frances Fyfield moves us closer to the legal technicalities attendant upon crime with her dauntless barrister Helen West and intrepid solicitor Sarah Fortune. But in terms of the cosseting predictabilities of the genre these new women detectives are little more than Miss Marples with strident political outlooks and active sex lives.

Minette Walters frequently shifts the narrative away from any obvious alliance with the state of mind of the investigator or perpetrator and attempts a form of documentary realism. Walters and Ruth Rendell (writing as Barbara Vine) also give attention to the psychology of crime; not the motivation of professional criminals, but the more perverse, obsessive causes of stalking, harassment, or unpremeditated assault. The virtuoso of this latter hybrid of crime writing and socio-psychology is Nicci French (actually the pairing of Nicci Gerard and Sean French) who began with *The Memory Game* (1996) and has produced fourteen similar novels up to and including *Complicit* (2009). More recently French's novels (from *Blue Monday*, 2011, to *Thursday's Children*, 2014) have focused on the experiences of the psychotherapist Frieda Klein, a women who proves to be a magnet for an extraordinary number of murderous psychopaths despite her wish to dissociate herself from criminology.

All of these are effective literary artists in their own right but their achievements are somewhat pallid in comparison with the crime novelist who continually created an unsettling amalgam between the enigma of pure evil and its compulsive attractions, Patricia Highsmith.

Christopher Brookmyre with *Quite Ugly One Morning* (1996) debuted as the Scottish version of Carl Hiaasen. The latter's novels are slapstick derivatives of the trend pioneered by Elmore Leonard with armed robbery and murderous intention as routine features of US daily life. This does not come across as particularly aberrant when set in Florida but Brookmyre's location is provincial Scotland and in all of his books, up to and including *When the Devil Drives* (2012), one senses that the battle between exhilaration and farce will always favour the latter. Mark Billingham (*Sleepyhead*, 2001 and *The Burning*

Girl, 2004), Frank Lean (*Above Suspicion*, 2001) and Ron Ellis (*Mean Streets*, 1999 and *Ears of the City*, 1998) all attempt to graft the nihilistic brutality of the US onto the urban environment of Britain, respectively North London, Manchester, and Liverpool. The mismatches are conspicuous. Billingham's DI Tom Thorne, Lean's Inspector David Cunane, and Ellis's retinue of policemen and private eyes strain toward various states of ruthless cynicism and debauchery, sufficient to match the ghastliness of their territories, but in each instance one senses an awkward exaggeration of character and setting; both seem at once absurd and incongruous.

Established novelists at the high end of the cultural spectrum frequently experiment with crime writing but one has the impression that they intend not so much to revivify the subgenre as to make use of its hidebound conventions as a background to their superior talents; in short, they are slumming. Martin Amis with *Night Train* (1997) has fun with standardized formulae, causing his narrator to be an evasive, unreliable US policewoman casually indifferent to a preponderance of noirish horrors and unable, in a fashionably postmodern manner, to resolve the case and therefore finish her story. Graham Swift in *The Light of Day* (2003) exploits the scaffolding of detective fiction for more earnest speculations on the human condition. Julian Barnes, disguised as Dan Kavanagh, during the first half of his career, published several amusing and occasionally thought-provoking novels involving the quixotic bisexual private eye Duffy (see *Fiddle City*, 1981 and *Putting the Boot In*, 1985) and one is caused to wonder if his early dalliance with the form played some part in the genesis of his celebrated Man Booker shortlisted piece *Arthur and George* (2005). Barnes raises questions about the very nature of detection, fabrication, and the pursuit of truth, using as he does a hall-of-mirrors procedure whereby he fictionalizes the creator of the world's best known detective while following a procedure and dealing with subjective emotional registers similar to those we associate with Doyle's creation, Holmes.

The British attempts to evolve a hybrid of crime and postmodern fiction seem conspicuously forced and incongruous compared, say, with their most celebrated US counterpart, Paul Auster's New York Trilogy (*City of Glass*, 1985; *Ghosts*, 1986; and *The Locked Room*, 1986). Auster does not so much deviate from as interrogate the lineage stretching from Raymond Chandler and Dashiell Hammett to Tom Wolfe, in which the routines of ordinary existence can suddenly become part of a deterministic nightmare outside the subject's and, as Auster indicates, the author's control. Crime writing in the US has for most of the 20th century been closely allied to its upmarket counterpart—realist and experimental—not because of some consensual indulgence on the part of the literary establishment but for the more straightforward reason that it reflects a fabric of experiences, mediated and actual, that most Americans take for granted. From the existence of organized crime—particularly the Mafia—as an element of the social and economic infrastructure through the acceptance of armed policemen and FBI agents as vigilantes and nemeses to a judicial system that is fundamentalist in its retributive zeal, crime is much closer to the routine mindset of ordinary Americans than it is to that of their British counterparts. This does not mean that America is on average a more dangerous place to be than the UK, but late 20th–early 21st century existence is composed to a large degree of secondary images and representations conveyed by film and the news media, and in this respect US readers encounter crime writing more as an extension of this experience than as a frightening excursion from it.

British writers who blur the distinction between good and evil or explore it fetishistically as a dimension of the creative spectrum are peculiarities, self-conscious deviants from a wholesome tradition. W. J. Burley's Cornwall-based 'Wycliffe' series, Peter Robinson's Yorkshire-based DCI Banks, John Harvey's Charlie Resnick of Nottingham, and more recently John Lawton's Chief

Superintendent Troy (*Blue Rondo*, 2005), Patrick Neate's Tommy Akhtar (*City of Tiny Lights*, 2005), Alexander McCall Smith's Isabel Dalhousie (*The Sunday Philosophy Club*, 2004) and Christopher Fowler's harmlessly quixotic Bryant and May of London's Peculiar Crimes Unit (*Seventy Seven Clocks*, 2005) are all permutations upon the basic design that gave us Morse, Frost, Dalziel, Rebus, et al. Even Michael Dibdin's endearingly amoral and eccentric Aurelio Zen, a man who regards villains with as much indulgence as he does the inefficient, corrupt Italian authorities to whom he answers, became an avuncular almost self-parodic version of his former presence.

The contrasts between P. D. James's *The Murder Room* (2003) and Arnott's *Truecrime* (2003) are fascinating. In the former, Dalgliesh seems little altered since his debut forty-one years earlier and his extracurricular interest in a 31-year-old Cambridge English lecturer, begun in a previous novel, ends with them agreeing that 'they might get to know each other'. Death and killing are attended to with equally respectful decorum—they seem, like sex, matters to be treated with solemnity and caution. James's style is consistently correct and elegant and even her low-life criminals seem able to maintain proper command of syntax, despite their other delinquencies. Arnott, on the other hand, abandons a commanding stylistic register in favour of the clipped, fragmentary mode that reflects the speech patterns and lifestyles of his characters. Morality and correctness exist but they seem constantly mutable, forever preyed upon by the unpredictabilities of a society with no agreed sense of order. As to the question of which more accurately reflects Britain at the close of the 20th century, the consensus would probably favour Arnott, but it should be remembered that crime fiction in all its manifestations involves a resolute perversion of actuality. All fiction is impressionistic; pure naturalistic accuracy is an ideal to be aspired to—by some—and never realized, but crime writing complicates matters by feeding upon the reader's least becoming inclinations.

A question remains, however, regarding the very different trajectories taken by British and American crime fiction since the 1960s. It could be argued that the latter has shifted more toward representations of the law and its agents as morally compromised, not in order to sell more books to readers with a taste for gratuitous violence, but rather because they are function as the collective conscience of an imperfect society. But does this mean that their more circumspect British counterparts prefer not to mention what they know or suspect (with the notable exception of figures such as Arnott and James)?

In Wambaugh's *Hollywood Station* (2006) we come across this passage.

> That was a bizarre event wherein a white sergeant, having shot Mr King with a taser gun after a long auto pursuit, then directed the beating of this drunken, drug-addled African American ex-convict. That peculiar sergeant seemed determined to make King cry uncle, when the ring of a dozen cops should have swarmed and handcuffed the drunken thug and been done with it.

The policeman who speaks these words is entirely fictitious but the event to which he refers, involving Rodney King, was very real. In 1991 King was beaten senseless by several Los Angeles police officers who were later charged and their acquittal triggered race riots there in 1992. Wambaugh's policeman shows no remorse; only a cynical disparagement for how his colleagues dealt with the 'drunken thug'. It is difficult to imagine that a contemporary British crime fiction writer would use, say, the murder of Stephen Lawrence to blend fact with fiction and present members of the Metropolitan Police, albeit invented ones, as casual racists.

Chapter 4
International crime fiction

France

The pioneers of crime fiction were British and US novelists, followed closely by the French. In Conan Doyle's *A Study in Scarlet* Holmes digresses from his immediate case to scoff at the French police, specifically a certain detective called Lecoq whom he describes as 'a miserable bungler'. That this fictitious figure echoes, in his name at least, the very real Eugène François Vidocq is no accident. Until 1809 Vidocq's life resembled the plot from an overwritten picaresque novel. He first went to prison aged 13, when his father decided to teach him a lesson and reported him to the authorities for his theft of much of the family's silverware. He served in the army on three occasions, deserting after each, and during the rest of his youth pursued an active career as womanizer, bigamist, burglar, duellist, and fraudster. He experienced four terms of imprisonment; he escaped first from hard labour in the galleys disguised as a sailor, next in a stolen nun's habit, and following this he took flight from detention in Toulon after bribing a prostitute to bring him women's clothing. In 1805 he was captured again, taken to Louvres and found that he had been sentenced to death in absentia. On 28 November he jumped out of a window into the adjacent river Scarpe. Four years later, shortly before his thirty-fourth birthday, he was arrested again and this time bought himself a form of leniency by convincing the court and the police that he knew more about the criminal fraternity, particularly in Paris, than they ever would and that as an informer, or *mouton*, he would enable them to have some impact upon the seemingly invulnerable gangsters of the French capital. He was so successful that in 1811 he was allowed to recruit and command a group of similarly reformed ex-criminals who provided the nucleus for what would officially be titled the *Brigade de la Sûreté*, effectively the first ever plain-clothes detective branch of a police force. He commanded the *Sûreté* until 1827 and is recognized as the father of modern criminology. Along with his direct knowledge of the practices and the mentality of criminals he perfected a system for indexing which enabled detectives to check their own instincts against documented facts about known suspects. He developed several chemical compounds which would both deter and counteract the forgery of cheques and promissory notes—crimes which he had practised with great success in his twenties—and crucially he perfected a methodology of crime scene investigations in which proof of a perpetrator's involvement could be presented by matching aspects of their physical or mental attributes with physical evidence. He even made the first advances into the science of ballistics, proving in the famous case of the Comtesse Isabelle d'Arcy that her husband was not her murderer. The bullet—which he persuaded a doctor to remove from her head in secret—matched the pistol of her lover, but was too large to have been discharged from the Comte's duelling pistol.

Vidocq published his memoirs (*Memoires de Vidocq, chef de la police de Sûreté, jusqu'en 1827*) a year after he resigned as head of the *Sûreté*. The book became an immediate bestseller partly because it read like a novel. He was unapologetic about his early life as a criminal and dealt with his later years as a detective in an un-self-righteous manner: he was less interested in the morality of the perpetrators of the crimes he solved than in the fascinating procedures of detection.

Poe is credited with inventing the modern crime novel with his short story 'The Murders in the Rue Morgue' but the accolade is founded on a technicality. Dupin is based on Vidocq. Certainly, Dupin moves up several classes beyond Vidocq's humble background and there is no hint that before becoming a detective he operated as a lawbreaker; Dupin is, as Poe's narrator describes him, 'of an excellent—indeed an illustrious family'. He is an aristocrat; arrogant, erudite, and apparently able to carry his powers of deduction to a point almost of omniscience. What impressed Poe most about Vidocq was his ability to assume such a vast range of disguises. As a detective he often deceived his suspects by seeming to be someone else and he encouraged recruits to the *Sûreté* to learn from and follow his example. Dupin does not resort to such crude methods as dressing to deceive, yet he borrows from Vidocq an air of the esoteric. Even his companion, the narrator of the stories, is puzzled by who he really is and, to an equal degree, is in awe of his ability to detect the truth from mysteries that all others find impenetrable. We never learn anything of how Dupin keeps himself financially. He is a private detective of sorts but not willing to descend to the vulgar state of expecting payment for his invaluable solutions—and in this respect Poe's character is a convenient perversion of Vidocq. While running the *Sûreté* the latter unashamedly hired himself out, sometimes along with his resources and employees, for private investigations; after his resignation he set up a detective agency, often working alongside representatives of the government or pursuing uncommissioned cases of his own—eventually, in 1842, he was arrested again, this time for embezzlement and kidnapping. Peel away the morally, culturally, and politically suspect features of Vidocq and another aspect of Dupin emerges: a man who regards himself as above the law, immune from the crude machinations of the state, and contemptuous of middle-class complacency.

During the years following his resignation from the *Sûreté* Vidocq met and became friendly with Honoré de Balzac, but we have no record of how he felt about Balzac's recreation of him as Vautrin in the novels of his *La Comédie Humaine* series. His most conspicuous and memorable appearance is in *Le Père Goriot* (1834/5). The novel begins in 1819 with the Restoration of the Bourbon monarchy. Its three main characters are Rastignac, scion of minor southern gentry who has come to Paris in the hope of rejoining the re-established aristocracy, Goriot, an elderly merchant who cares only for the well-being of his horribly selfish daughters, and Vautrin, master of disguise, perpetrator of numerous crimes, and, under his real name Jacques Collin, the subject of several police investigations. Vautrin is one of the most puzzling figures in literature. He encourages Rastignac's ambitions, specifically by urging him to court and marry Victorine. There will, he advises him, be few competitors since Victorine's considerable family fortune is destined for her brother, but, he adds, he can arrange for the latter to be killed in a duel. Rastignac is horrified and the most significant and controversial episode in the novel is when Vautrin attempts to convince his acquaintance that advancing oneself financially and socially must involve the visitation of distress, death included, on others. At one point he informs him that 'the secret of a great success for which you are at a loss to account is a crime that has never been discovered, because it was properly executed'. Most commentators on the novel regard this as a candid account of social and financial advancement: success involves a crime against the well-being of others.

The novel is important because it provides an example of the trajectory that crime fiction might have taken shortly after its emergence as a subgenre in the mid-19th century. It is treated unquestioningly as an example of classic realism, the sort of book that holds a mirror up to society without trying to obscure its vile injustices: Marx and Engels were outspoken fans of Balzac. Look closer, however, and one detects the definitive aspects of crime writing: murder inspired by ambition, clandestine criminality, and the question of whether the authorities will intervene or apprehend the offender. Certainly, these feature as only a small element of the novel's fabric but they are without doubt the most memorable. 'Rastignac' became synonymous in French with the notion of a person willing to climb the social ladder at all costs and Vautrin remains a mysterious figure in that it is impossible to decide on whether he embodies amoral criminality or acts as a sagacious commentator on a society that is beyond redemption—in this respect it is clear that Balzac was fascinated by his model, Vidocq's, ability to switch personae and evade easy classification. Vautrin's shadowy, elusive presence reflects the enigma of the book itself. It is not the kind of documentary or dystopian realism practised later by the likes of Zola and Orwell; rather it combines an unsparingly naturalistic portrait of society with an exciting crime thriller. When it was published, however, the latter was still at an embryonic stage in its development; it would be six years until Poe brought out his first short story.

Balzac's experiment indicated that crime, police detection, and the workings of the judiciary might both capture the attention of the ordinary reader and encapsulate key elements of the realist project; crime fiction, as we now understand it, might have become a respectable adjunct to the literary novel. Others toyed with this premise: the reformed criminal Jean Valjean and Police Inspector Javert of Hugo's *Les Misérables* (1862) were modelled on Vidocq as was the *Sûreté* detective Monsieur Jackal in Dumas's *Les Mohicans de Paris* (1854–9). But the promise offered by each would be extinguished by Emile Gaboriau (1832–73). His first novel, *L'Affaire Lerouge* (1865), featured a detective called Le Père Tabaret, an unashamed borrowing from Poe's Dupin, and by implication from the very real Vidocq. Thereafter his fiction was dominated by the presence of Monsieur Lecoq, a police detective without a Christian name and once again modelled on Vidocq. Lecoq too is a reformed criminal-turned-*Sûreté* detective. Significantly, Gaboriau is unconcerned with Vidocq/Lecoq as an unwitting avatar of the endemic inequalities and hypocrisies of French society. He is more interested in the complex and ingenious methods of detection that Vidocq described in his memoirs.

Lecoq is possessed of an almost superhuman capacity to decode the motives and techniques of murderers and eventually to unmask the perpetrator of the crime. Gaboriau, with thanks to Vidocq, offers the reader a lesson in logic and deduction; on how a sequence of apparently unrelated clues and events can be shown to be a narrative of motivation, cause, action, and eventually disclosure. In this respect he provided a bridge between Poe and Conan Doyle. The latter saw himself as the worthy successor to Poe but his proper inspiration came from Gaboriau's Lecoq whose methods of detection are replicated by Holmes. The latter's disparaging reference to Lecoq as 'bungling' is, one assumes, a backhanded compliment and acknowledgement of his assistance.

After Gaboriau the police detective took leave of absence from the French crime novel, at least until the 1930s. It is assumed that his departure reflected a general opinion that from the second Republic onwards the police were by parts agents of oppressive political regimes and endemically corrupt. Instead, we come across figures such as the investigative journalist Joseph Rouletabille who in Gaston Leroux's *The Mystery of the Yellow Chamber* (1907) treats the police with contempt and advertises his own deductive skills in solving such mysteries as how a fatally injured woman could be found in a room securely locked from the inside. Leroux is another example of the curious relationship between British and French crime fiction. Rouletabille and his companion-narrator are a remodelling of Holmes and Watson but the structure of the novel—based on a group of bourgeois individuals seemingly detached from the rest of the world, all of whom have something to hide and who offer the reader the equivalent of a narrative crossword puzzle—was later acknowledged by Agatha Christie as influencing her trademark 'country house' mysteries. John Dickson Carr also disclosed that Leroux had inspired some of his work.

Maurice Leblanc's Arsène Lupin is a roguish and glamorous gentleman who invites comparison with Holmes but differs from him in appealing to the blend of patriotism and self-loathing that gripped the French middle classes in the early years of the 20th century (he first appeared in a short story in the magazine *Je Sais Tout*, in July 1904 and continued to appear in print through the First World War and until the 1930s). Lupin funds his amateur lifestyle by stealing from wealthy members of the middle and upper classes, but Leblanc makes it clear that his victims have acquired their wealth by vulgar and sometimes illegal means and therefore deserve their fate. Many of his mysteries involve the uncovering of attempts by agents of the regime of Kaiser Wilhelm to undermine the stability of France: long before a World War became a realistic prospect the French establishment cultivated a deep contempt for Germany, inspired by their ignominious defeat by Bismarck in the 1870s.

As an antidote to the assumption that the habits of French crime writing—for authors and readers alike—were predictable we should compare Lupin with his successor Fantômas (originally co-authored by Marcel Allain and Pierre Souvestre until the latter's death in 1914) who first went into print in 1911 and can claim to be the most durable of all crime fiction characters; the final novel in the Fantômas series, *Fantômas Mène le Bal*, came out in 1963, six years before Allain's death. He can also be treated as the first to overturn the moral proprieties of the genre. Like Lupin he is a gentleman-thief, though he shows no interest in solving crimes committed by others. Fantômas is a serial seducer who abandons the considerable number of women, mostly aristocratic, he makes pregnant; he commits murder without a hint of remorse and seems motivated mainly by a macabre sadistic pleasure in visiting fear and destruction on his victims—he displays a particular taste for strangling and beheading them. The only thing he has in common with Lupin is an apparent disdain for the police, who are presented as buffoons in their attempts to apprehend him. His adventures sometimes seem designed to defy credibility—he poses as a German Archduke, has an affair with a British duchess, plays havoc in America, Mexico, and India, and fights in the Boer War. One can only assume that the authors injected this air of improbability into his work to relieve the reader of potential feelings of guilt: Fantômas stimulated grotesque and unseemly fantasies too absurd to be treated as actual cravings.

Respectability returned to the mainstream crime writing tradition with the publication of *The Strange Case of Peter the Lett* (1931) written by the Belgian, Georges Simenon (Figure 3), but based on the activities of a senior detective in the Paris *Préfecture*, Jules Maigret. Today the Maigret novels seem worthily orthodox, and to an extent they are, but when they first went into print they were unprecedented. Before World War II police detectives in British, American, or indeed French crime novels were either subordinates to the amateur or private investigator or morally ambiguous curiosities. Maigret was the first to embody a sturdy middle-class respect for the law and the judicial system. He often proves able to think like the criminals he pursues but he never crosses the line from his own world of inflexible values and integrity to their sphere of criminality. He was the first fictional detective to offer the reader a reassuring, avuncular presence; the sort of policeman we hope will come to our aid if lawlessness disturbs our existence.

From the 1940s onwards the French version of the subgenre continued to offer eccentric alternatives to its British and American counterparts. Léo Malet's Nestor Burma sometimes resembles the hard-boiled heroes of Chandler's books except that his explorations of different districts of Paris are touched with hints of the surreal. He first appeared in 1943 and Malet's perversions of actuality might be taken as a comment on the Occupation.

San Antonio (the pseudonym of Frédéric Dard) pioneered a version of crime fiction unmatched in Britain and the US and

3. Georges Simenon. 'When I went to visit [Gide] I always saw my
books with so many notes in the margins that they were almost more
Gide than Simenon. I never asked him about them; I was very shy about
it. So now I will never know.' (Simenon in *The Paris Review*, 1955)

generally untranslatable: the narrative, not only the dialogue, is dominated by the often impenetrable patois of the regional proletariat and the criminal underworld.

Boileau-Narcejac (the nom de plume of Pierre Boileau and Thomas Narcejac) pioneered fictional investigations of disturbed, sometimes criminally inclined psychological states and are better known from their film adaptations than from translations. They produced the prototype stories for Hitchcock's *Vertigo* and Clouzet's *Les Diaboliques*.

Far more than in Britain and the US, the rural provinces of France, along with the country's provincial cities, provide not only the setting but inform the texture of much post-1950s crime writing. Provence and the Côte d'Azur are particular favourites (see Pierre Magnan, Michel Grisolia, Jean-Claude Izzo, and Maurice Périsset), and Maurice Bastide uncovers convincing layers of criminality beneath the elegance of Bordeaux and the bordering vineyards. René Belletto introduces us to the gangsters of Lyon and Philippe Huet (Normandy) and Hervé Jaouen (Brittany) disclosed uncomfortable activities in the seemingly idyllic north-western areas of the French countryside.

Finally, I must give some attention to France's most famous, internationally-bestselling contemporary crimewriter, Fred Vargas (real name, Frédérique Audoin-Rouzeau), for no better reason than she is virtually impossible to categorize. She said in an interview with the *Guardian* (18 January 2004) that she feels more of an affiliation to British crime fiction than with US writing or with her French peers or predecessors. Her statement flatters the work of her northern neighbours: there are parallels, certainly, but they are outweighed by contrasts. Her main characters—such as the medieval historian Marc Vandoosler and Police Commissaire Jean-Baptiste Adamsberg—are magnificently eccentric and her plots often turn upon events that carry an air of the surreal (a tree planted anonymously in someone's garden or a severed toe discovered in dog-mess on a Paris pavement, for example) but, throughout, an undertow of menace pulls us back towards a world in which murders are indeed committed. Imagine, if you can, a Gallic hybrid of Borges, P. D. James, and Julian Barnes and you will come close to appreciating her uniqueness.

Iberia and Italy

Crime fiction in France was and is far more popular, diverse, and dynamic than in any other nation in continental Europe. For example, in Italy during the 19th century the only home-grown alternatives to untranslated British and American works were novels that more closely resembled religious fables than genuine crime thrillers, often with the guilty person known from the outset and the focus remaining on the moral reverberations of the act. Typical of this form of writing was Francesco Mastriani's *My Corpse* and *The Blind Woman From Sorrento* (both 1852), Cletto Arrighi's *The Black Hand* (1883), and Emilio de Marchi's *The Priest's Hat* (1858). In 1910 the newspaper *Il Corriere della Sera* began to publish in serial form translations of Conan Doyle's short stories and this marked the beginning of a widespread interest in Poe, Gaboriau, Leroux, and Souvestre and Allain. *I Libri gialli* (Yellow Books) was founded in 1929 and began by publishing only translations of French, British, and American writers, but in 1931 it brought out Varaldo's *Seven is Beautiful*, thought to be the first mainstream Italian crime novel; it featured Police Inspector Ascenio Borichi, who bears a close resemblance to Gaboriau's Inspector Lecoq. The newly installed Fascist regime ruled that at least 20 per cent of the Yellow Press's output must come from Italian writers and while this ordinance encouraged participation it limited range severely by also demanding that the fictional perpetrators of serious crimes must not be Italians. A number of writers found a loophole in this by setting their work abroad—Ezio D'Errico, imitating Simenon, set his work in France and Giorgio Scerbanenco took his to Boston, Massachusetts—but this rather farcical exercise in censorship was brought to an end in 1941 when Mussolini's Ministry of Culture banned the publication of all types of crime fiction, claiming that it corrupted the young and encouraged a general tendency towards immorality. After the war the two trends that still dominate Italian crime fiction were set by Giorgio Scerbanenco, who adapted the American 'noir' amateur detective mode to the underworld of Milan, and Carlo Emilio Gadda who in 1946 published *That Awful Mess on Via Merulana*. It is set in the late 1920s at the inception of Fascism and combines harsh social realism with a cynical presentation of the judicial establishment, the police in particular. The best known more recent version of the former is Andrea Camilleri's Inspector Montalbano series, based on the experiences of a fractious Sicily-based detective as much interested in food as in solving crime. Gadda's most important successor is Leonardo Sciascia, who also bases his novels in Sicily, offering a picture of how Mafia-based criminality informs all aspects of society, particularly the police and judiciary.

In Spain, Pedro Antonio Alarcón's *The Nail and Other Tales of Mystery and Crime* (1853) appeared more than half a century before Emilia Pardo Bazan's *A Drop of Blood* but the latter is treated by most as Spain's first crime novel, and then with some scepticism. Alarcón's 'The Nail' is a first person account by a male stage-coach passenger of his encounter with a woman who is eventually found guilty of her husband's murder. The nail of the title is embedded in the skull of his disinterred corpse. She confesses, and after being sentenced to death, announces gnomically that while she killed him another man was responsible for the act. A horseman arrives with a pardon minutes before her execution and her earlier statement of innocence remains an enigma. It is an impressive story not least because the narrator is caught between the roles of involuntary detective and puzzled observer. We leave it much as he does: unsettled and fascinated. It belongs in that category of stories written in the early to mid-19th century when crime fiction was a genre without clear conventions and all the more fascinating for that. Bazan, conversely, borrows much from the thriving British and French tradition of the gentleman amateur detective, a person whose considerable deductive skills flatter those readers who regard themselves as equally well equipped to unravel the mysteries of the crime.

As with Italy, the early years of the 20th century saw Conan Doyle, Poe, and other acknowledged masters of the form translated into Spanish and their mannerisms imitated by indigenous writers. For example Joaquin Belda published *Who Shot?*, involving a version of Holmes and Watson based in Spain; their presence is so incongruous that the book reads as an unwitting caricature.

The Civil War and the subsequent Franco dictatorship effectively extinguished crime writing in Spain for more than a generation. A few so-called 'police procedurals' were published but each was an elegy to the untarnished probity and efficiency of the police force; crimes are solved and criminals apprehended with textbook predictability. It had become clear to authors that anything else would be banned by Franco's censors. Francisco García Pavón is probably the best-known state-indulged crime writer of this period.

After Franco, crime writing in Spain celebrated its new-found freedom with a shift towards generally left-wing radicalism. Andrew Martin, a Catalan, produced during the 1970s seven violent novels based on the activities of the Barcelona police, who have exchanged authoritarianism for corruption. The best-known, most widely celebrated post-Franco writer is Manuel Vázquez Montalbán. Imprisoned and tortured during the 1960s for publishing subversive articles, Vázquez Montalbán exacted a form of revenge in the invention of Pepe Carvalho. The Carvalho series spans two decades and twenty-two novels from 1981 to 2003, and its anti-hero, based mainly in Barcelona, an erstwhile communist and CIA agent turned police detective, provides a cynical perspective on a greedy, ruthless society.

Central and Eastern Europe

The history of crime fiction in Germany and Russia returns us to the question of how the genre might have developed had it not become dominated by the techniques of Collins, Poe, and Conan Doyle. Friedrich Schiller's 'Der Verbrecher aus verlorener Ehre' ('The Criminal From Lost Honour') (1786) might well lay claim to be the first ever example of crime fiction were it not for its refusal to be classified either as crime writing or anything else. It opens with a dry reflection on the nature of crime and we have no reason to suspect that the speaker is not Schiller himself offering us a philosophical treatise, but then he introduces us to the story of one Christian Wolf, son of a rural innkeeper. His initial account of Wolf's descent into criminality, specifically poaching, seems like a heavy-handed anticipation of Freudianism, an example of pseudo-psychology not uncommon during the Enlightenment; but soon Wolf begins to dominate the narrative, his reported speech pushing the narrator's comments into the margins. Schiller, or his proxy, never quite disappears but for the bulk of the story we are mesmerized by what seems a successful takeover of the narrative by one of its subjects, and equally fascinated by a shift away from a factual description towards a mystifying short story. Wolf kills a man who seems likely to challenge him for the attention of a particular woman and we follow the former in his flight through the forest and in his encounter with a band of criminal renegades. Questions abound (for example, how does the initial narrator have such an intense understanding of Wolf's motives and feelings of fear and guilt?), and had it not been published in 1786 it would surely qualify as an example of postmodern crime fiction.

Just as puzzling is E. T. A. Hoffmann's *Fräulein von Scuderi* (1819). The novel is set in 17th century Paris and includes a number of characters based on real figures from the reign of Louis XIV. The eponymous Fräulein is a version of the poetess

Madeleine de Scudéry and another figure in the novel, La Reynie, appears to be based on Gabriel Nicolas de la Regnie, who was commissioned by Louis XIV to organize what was Europe's first police force, effectively a paramilitary unit whose principal role was to protect merchants, gentry, and the aristocracy from the rampant villainy of the Parisian underclass. Hoffmann evokes all of this but soon his story begins to spiral away from recorded history, presenting Paris as a city besieged by gangs of thieves and in a state of collective paranoia. The criminals seem able to target their victims not only because of the latter's apparent wealth: they pay particular attention to men en route to presenting their mistresses and lovers with gifts of fine jewellery; though the questions of how the criminals identify such individuals and why they specifically target them remain unanswered. Many of them are killed and one has to wonder if Hoffmann is hinting that their murderers are agents of some form of natural justice.

The baroque complexity of the plot makes it immune from summary but what should be noted is that Scuderi is cast in the role of what would later be seen as the amateur detective, though her involvement is involuntary and somewhat distracted. A mysterious young man sends her enigmatic messages and he eventually turns out to be Olivier Brusson, assistant to the celebrated and recently murdered goldsmith René Cardillac. The novel is generally dismissed as a contender for classification as a pre-Collins and Poe inaugurator of crime fiction because Scuderi's role seems to be more that of intermediary than deductive investigator. She considers testimony from many involved, makes a plea to the king on Brusson's behalf, and eventually discloses to the former a confession made to her by the real killer, a member of the king's Guard called Moissens. But aside from her generous wish to see justice done and her willingness to intervene she does not actively solve the mystery. Conversely, however, one might argue that Hoffmann is pioneering a brand of realistic crime fiction—capturing as he does the degrees of power and influence that determine the fate of individuals in 17th century France—rather than creating the escapist illusion of someone, a detective, possessed of an almost magical ability to make sense of an insoluble conundrum.

With Schiller and Hoffmann the criminal act becomes a springboard for the investigation of more fundamental social and psychological issues while retaining the factor that would ensure the popularity of mainstream crime writing, excited fascination. For a novel which maintains this balance in the most extraordinary and accomplished manner we must move east. To treat Fyodor Dostoevsky's *Crime and Punishment* (1866) as a crime novel, despite its title, would these days be seen by most as an act of interpretative vulgarity. It has become, by consensus, a literary classic, a ground-breaking investigation of existential torment produced half a century before the Modernists began to venerate such topics.

Raskolnikov murders the pawnbroker Ivanovna, and her half-sister Lizaveta, without any clear motive. Rather, he indicates that some power beyond his control impels him to commit the act. Thereafter all of the other characters are in various ways drawn into Raskolnikov's emotional and moral nightmare of guilt, fear, and remorse, with one exception. Porfiry Petrovich, the detective in charge of investigating the murders, can be regarded as the most balanced, disinterested figure in the novel. Commentators tend to treat Petrovich as a marginal figure and in doing so they overlook his significance. Sonia, prostitute and Raskolnikov's confessor, is often regarded as invoking Mary Magdalene, albeit with nihilistic undertones. His sister Avdovita and Pulkheria his mother are treated as foils to the other important figure who sympathizes with Raskolnikov's plight, his friend Razumikhin-Svidrigailov, philanderer and possible mass murderer, who invites comparisons with Raskolnikov; it is as if Dostoevsky is asking us to rank each on a spectrum between evil and psychological imbalance. Raskolnikov and his crime act as magnets for virtually all the other characters in the novel, causing every one of them to in some way imitate the imbalance between the rational and the impulsive that inspired the murder. Petrovich, however, remains uniquely immune from this. In many respects he is a version of Poe's Dupin, except that Dostoevsky's reader shares the knowledge and plight of the perpetrator and the other figures drawn into his web, and we contemplate the calculating psychological games played by the detective. Instead of following the detective in his attempts to solve a mystery we become complicit in the complex atmosphere of moral ambiguity and threatened sanity generated by the murder and, more significantly, we know who committed it. *Crime and Punishment* indicates that the concept of crime, indeed the criminal act, could have become an important catalyst for a fictional exploration of more complex issues. While Poe, Collins, and Conan Doyle are routinely regarded as the inaugurators of the crime fiction template, they were, perhaps, also responsible for placing several limitations on its range.

This suspicion might have inspired another Russian writer savagely to satirize Poe and Collins in a short story first published in 1883. In Anton Chekhov's 'The Swedish Match' Inspector Dyukovsky bases his shocking disclosures on an apparently irrelevant piece of evidence, specifically the identification of a match dropped at the scene of the murder as Swedish in origin. His findings seem conclusive, drawing a confession from the person who purchased a box of Swedish matches, but as the narrative continues Dyukovsky comes to resemble an early prototype for Blake Edwards's film character Inspector Clouseau, and we also detect uncomfortable similarities with Dupin, in that both seem obsessed with finding seemingly preposterous connections between the inconsequential and the logical.

The post-Revolution civil war in Russia and the subsequent Bolshevik government inspired a unique blend of Western detective fiction and communist propaganda. Typically Marietta Shaginian, using the pseudonym Dzhim (Jim) Dollar, produced

Mess Mend: Yankees in Petrograd (1923). Her hero is Mike Thingmaster, part detective/part revolutionary, who recruits workers to a secret organization dedicated to solving the global 'crime' of world capitalism. Shaginian and other writers who followed her example attained immense popularity, at least until the death of Lenin. Stalin condemned her work as decadent fantasy. He went on to classify all crime fiction as a form of pro-Western escapism and banned the genre in its entirety.

In Nazi Germany the genre suffered a similar fate under the jurisdiction of Josef Goebbels, Hitler's Minister of Propaganda: any indication that criminality existed in the Third Reich was seen as a critique of the ideal of Aryan integrity. The work of only two significant crime writers survived the Nazi regime. Erich Kästner's *Emil and the Detectives* (1929) remained in print throughout this period, as did Norbert Jacques's series of 'Dr Mabuse' novels, first published during the 1920s. It is likely that Goebbels's censors treated Kästner's story of a gang of schoolboy detectives abroad in Berlin as a harmless children's story and Jacques's creation, who resembles Fantômas, as a similarly innocuous fantasy. In truth both carry sinister allegorical messages about Germany on the brink of its descent towards fascism.

Most post-war German writers and post-Soviet Russians adapted contemporaneous US models to their particular social and cultural milieu. Victor Dotsenko's heroes come across as versions of Rambo, one being an Afghan veteran who wreaks bloodthirsty havoc on the Moscow Mafia, while Aleksandra Marinina's Lt Colonel Anastasia Kamenskaya taps into a pervasive feeling of nostalgia for the days when the State-backed 'People's Militia' kept the city in good order. Kamenskaya is a ruthless administrator who has no time for such Western indulgences as feminism and has earned herself three very popular adaptations for series on Russian television.

A number of German and Austrian writers made commendable attempts to reconcile the populist element of crime writing with philosophical themes and contemporary realism. Heimito von Doderer's *Every Man a Murderer* (1938) brings Dostoevsky into a mid-20th century context. It escaped the attention of Goebbels's censors because it does not conform to the Anglo-American formula of crime writing. The main character's concern with the apparent murder of his sister-in-law gradually draws us away from the question of who killed her to the more disturbing issue of his obsession with the act. The most celebrated example of a German writer dragging the crime genre into the sphere of mainstream literary fiction is found in the Nobel Prize-winner Heinrich Böll's *The Lost Honour of Katherine Blum* (1974). Blum confesses to killing the journalist Tötges but we are troubled less by whether she is telling the truth or what motivated her than by the burgeoning unavoidable question of whether, in her circumstances, we too would have killed him, without much remorse.

Globally, crime fiction falls into two categories: those writers who adapted their work to the techniques first developed by Poe, Collins, and Conan Doyle and perfected during the 'Golden Age'; and those who attempted to remodel the genre, often prompted by historical and cultural legacies that bore little resemblance to those of Britain or America. Writers in the first category outnumber considerably those in the second.

East Asia

Tales of magistrates and the workings of the judicial system first became popular during the Song Imperial dynasty of China between the 10th and 13th centuries. In some ways these resembled the 18th century *Newgate Calendar* in that there was no question about the identity of the perpetrator; instead the reader's taste for the macabre was satiated. Yet some time before the demise of the Manchu dynasty in 1912 and the foundation of a Republic, translations of Poe and Conan Doyle were becoming immensely popular. In the early years of the Republic writers such as Cheng

Xiaoqing and Sun Liaohong produced what amounted to China-based replicas of Holmes and Dupin. From 1945 until the death of Mao in 1976 conventional detective fiction of this kind was banned; it was thought to encourage an unhealthy interest in a society whose decadent excesses, and consequent tendency towards criminality, were already well documented. A version of the magistrate-focused novel was revived under Mao's successor Deng Xiaoping, but mainly as a means of rewriting recent history. Most pieces were set in the Maoist era, depicting a corrupt police force and incompetent judiciary (the only collection in English is *The Wounded*, translated by G. Barnes and B. Lee).

Since China opened itself to a globalized, largely capitalist trading network the crime novel has not so much thrived as made tentative claims to independence in a state which still exerts tight controls on its printed and electronic media. The one exception is Wang Shuo, who rose to prominence, and was thereafter subject to frequent bans, with *Playing For Thrills* (1989). The narrator Fang Yen might well have committed a murder but such is his drunken dissolute lifestyle, even he can't be certain of his guilt or innocence. He comes across as a rather endearing, if feckless and potentially dangerous, late 20th century version of Raskolnikov. The novel caused controversy in China not least because Yen and his friends conduct themselves in the kind of shambolic, hedonistic manner that we routinely associate with Western youth culture.

Aside from a few stories by the 17th century poet Ihara Saikaku, involving the crime-solving abilities of the Samurai, crime fiction was absent from Japanese writing until, as in China, versions of European stories and novels went into translation. Ruiko Kuroiwa's 'Three Strands of Hair' (1889) carries the formulaic imprint of Gaboriau into a Japanese context, but the acknowledged founder of modern Japanese crime fiction is Taro Hirai whose pseudonym was a clear enough statement of his debt to Western tradition. Edogawa Rampo, if rapidly pronounced with attention to a blend of Anglo-Japanese phonetics, is a rendering of Edgar Allan Poe. Rampo recreated a Japanese version of Dupin, the principal difference being that Rampo's tales offer sub-plots involving a level of sexual explicitness and deviancy that would not have been countenanced in Britain and the US until the end of the 1960s. As early as 1925, for example, in 'Case of Murder on the D-Slope' as much attention is given to the nature of the victim's sadomasochistic extramarital affair as to her demise.

Rampo's tendency to blend the purist European model of crime fiction with less predictable elements of the human social and psychological mindset endures in post-war Japanese writing. *A Wild Sheep Chase* (1982) by Haruki Murakami is one of the most bizarre crime novels ever produced. The unnamed, chain-smoking main character is following a man through Tokyo and the style of the opening perfectly replicates the seedy tension of James M. Cain's novels. We expect to find that the man pursued is in some way involved in something furtive and conspiratorial, a crime whose nature and repercussions will be unpicked with the unfolding of the narrative. Instead, however, the detective is persuaded to take charge of a hunt for a sheep that has not been seen for years. The question of why the missing animal creates concern among so many apparently sane individuals is not even addressed let alone answered and things become even more bizarre as the Holmes-like figure is distracted by an encounter with a woman with magically seductive ears and a man who dresses like a sheep. The conventions of a Conan Doyle story are invoked but the work is not a parody; rather we find that the improbable or peculiar aspects of classical crime writing (and here we should remember that in Poe's first story the crime was committed by an ape) that we are accustomed to take for granted or overlook are restored to their proper degree of strangeness.

Miyuki Miyabe's first novel *All She Was Worth* (1992) begins with police detective Shunsuke Honma hired for a private investigation into the disappearance of his nephew's fiancée, but what seems to be a standard narrative involving kidnap and possibly murder mutates into a meditation on how a society obsessed with credit and lending can gradually erode a person's sense of identity, to the point of extinction.

Latin America

For a region that seems collectively determined to forswear transatlantic conventions we should turn our attention to South America. Paul Graussac was the first Argentine crime novelist and his short story 'The Golden Lock' suggested that indigenous writers would follow European precedent; Graussac's story was effectively Dupin transplanted to Buenos Aires. Similarly, Horacio Quirogna, a native Uruguayan writing in and about Argentina, created in *The Exiles* a Latin American version of Collins's Sergeant Cuff. The first signs of change came with the launch of a series of stories in 1942 when H. Bustos Domecq published *Six Problems for Don Isidro Parodi*. Domecq was the pseudonym for two writers, Jorge Luis Borges and Adolfo Bioy-Casares, who co-authored these pieces. The stories, which Domecq contrived to produce intermittently for the subsequent three decades, are treated by some as parodies of virtually all aspects of the 'Golden Age' mode of fiction writing; detectives are by varying degrees petulant, incompetent, and distracted and the crimes themselves often seem to blend the macabre with the farcical. Equally, however, one might regard them as the first attempt to combine the standard conventions of crime fiction with magic realism, fifty years before Martin Amis's *Night Train* and Paul Auster's *New York Trilogy*.

In the same year, 1942, Borges began to publish crime stories under his own name. The first, 'Death and the Compass', tells of how a police detective, Lonnrot, investigates the murder of a rabbi in an unnamed city that any Argentine reader would recognize as Buenos Aires. Another death occurs and the perpetrator leaves messages, based on the Tetragrammaton, indicating when and where the next homicide will occur. Throughout, Borges continually shifts the balance between stark realism and chimerical fable. If anything resembling a clear intention can be identified, it is in Borges's nuanced reflection of a society where matters such as the real, the fabulous, and the horribly fatal shift restlessly in and out of focus.

Many Argentine writers followed Borges's example. Manuel Peyrou's *Thunder of Roses* (1948) carries hints of parody and blends these brilliantly with an otherwise dystopian atmosphere redolent of Dostoevsky's Russia. Juan Carlos Onetti matches Borges as an innovative practitioner of the genre and Manuel Puig's novels of the 1970s and 80s are darkly inconclusive, sexual, and surreal, evoking a brand of pessimism that reaches beyond the specific crime towards a general sense of fear; at the time Argentina was in the grip of a ruthless military dictatorship. The dangers of allowing violent fiction to directly reflect a murderously authoritarian society became evident when Rodolfo Jorge Walsh turned his novels into commentaries on the variously corrupt and dictatorial regimes of the 1950s onwards (his *Operation Massacre*, 1957, was based on a state-sponsored massacre). In 1977 he was abducted by the authorities and murdered.

Argentine crime fiction returns us emphatically to a question addressed elsewhere in this chapter, and raises another. First, do certain societies and cultures encourage aberrations from the classical tradition of Poe, Conan Doyle, and the Golden Age? If so, do the novels and stories which result from this provide evidence that crime writing can rise above its subordinate state as popular, non-literary writing? This last issue will be considered in Chapter 7.

Scandinavia

Before closing this chapter, some attention should be given to a recent phenomenon that is both overwhelming and, for most, inexplicable: the mass market preoccupation among readers in Britain and America with Scandinavian crime writing. Novels by Henning Mankell featuring the detective Kurt Wallander have sold forty million copies worldwide, the vast majority being translations into English. There are twelve authors from, variously, Norway, Sweden, Denmark, Iceland, and Finland who have each topped the bestseller lists in the US and the UK with sales of more than one million per novel. To understand why a region not previously known for its detective fiction should suddenly galvanize readers in the heartlands of the genre, we should consider the image of Scandinavia, particularly Sweden and Norway, that has endured elsewhere since the 1950s. For most, especially in the UK, Scandinavian countries epitomize the ideals of equanimity and institutionalized civility that many advanced European states aspired to in the decades after World War II. Supplement this with cities that seem havens of calm and rural environments made up of small communities founded on the principles of good citizenship and one has a group of nation states guaranteed to provoke a mixture of envy and admiration abroad, particularly among the left-leaning intelligentsia.

There is certainly no evidence that any of the successful Scandinavian writers calculatedly exploited the region's international profile, but it becomes clear that the contrast between the setting and the nature of the crimes depicted and investigated was the principal reason for the popularity of the books. Typically the sixth novel in Mankell's Wallander series, *The Fifth Woman* (1996), opens in a seemingly idyllic village community, home to a reclusive poet whose body is discovered in a ditch, horrifically impaled upon a sharpened bamboo pole and partially consumed by crows. The next victim is the owner of the local flower shop whose demise is, the perpetrator ensures, hideously slow and painful. A relatively recent newcomer to this festival of the gruesome is the Norwegian writer Anne Holt whose *What Never Happens* (2004) might lay claim to being one of the most macabre pieces of fiction ever written. The victims are members of the Oslo social and cultural establishment and each dies quite hideously: a talk show host's tongue is cut out, a politician crucified with a copy of the Koran stuffed inside her, and a major literary critic stabbed in the brain via their eye socket.

In these and in the work of Camilla Lackberg, Jo Nesbø, and Stieg Larsson we encounter settings, collective states of mind, that most would treat as unostentatiously civilized; societies and citizens content with themselves and their achievements. The contexts are inversely related to the savagery, sometimes the motiveless nihilistic cruelty, of the murders, and the reader's feelings of shock are proportionately intensified. To an extent we can trace the ancestry of such effects back to the settings of Christie and her peers where complacent middle-class worlds are disturbed by something disagreeable and fatal. But the Scandinavian writers make full use of the non-Nordic reader's often idealized perception of their society to cause the shattering of expectations to become all the more brutal. In this regard they can also be treated as distant relatives of the Sensation novels and the American 'noir' works of the mid-20th century, catering as they do for a less than commendable taste for the macabre; that which is enjoyed from a distance by the uninvolved spectator.

Chapter 5
Gender

Victorian writing

The history of women in crime novels both as authors and characters is closely paralleled by the record of how gender has featured in fiction as a whole.

Virginia Woolf, in *A Room of One's Own* (1929), addressed the question of why there are more pre-20th century women novelists than poets and claimed that 'the novel alone was young enough to be soft in [their] hands'. More recently the critics Sandra Gilbert and Susan Gubar elaborated on this and professed that the novel enables the woman to disguise herself, operate anonymously, even passively, as the creator of characters and choreographer of their actions.

This goes some way to explain why in the 18th and 19th centuries the novel encouraged participation by more women writers than the male-dominated genre of verse but a question remains as to why there are so few—in truth, less than five—women crime writers before the early 20th century Golden Age. Their scarcity becomes even more puzzling when we compare crime fiction with the Gothic novel. During the late 18th and 19th centuries the most popular women Gothic novelists outnumbered their male counterparts, with Ann Radcliffe, Charlotte Dacre, Elizabeth Gaskell, Louisa May

Alcott, Elizabeth Helme, Isabella Kelly, Mary Meeke, and Elizabeth Sleath contributing to what could be treated as the first predominantly female genre in Anglophone literature. There are numerous reasons for this, the most obvious being that the scenarios and narratives of Gothic writing charted largely unreal territories and as a consequence there was no obvious mismatch between conservative notions of what women could do in the real world and their role as creators of an ostentatiously fantastic fictional version. It seems strange, therefore, that crime writing did not provide a similarly attractive creative niche for women writers, given that it too involved a form of escapism. Indeed Poe's early career as a Gothic novelist is often treated as the inspiration for the peculiar world of Inspector Dupin.

Mary Elizabeth Braddon's *Lady Audley's Secret* (1862) is the first detective novel by a woman in Britain or America. Its classification as 'Sensation' fiction is due largely to Braddon's shameless replication of key elements of the real-life Constance Kent case of 1860 which held the attention of newspaper readers of all classes for several years. Lady Audley does not commit any serious crime, at least until the conclusion when fear of exposure drives her to attempted arson, but as the narrative unfolds she is exposed as guilty of an offence that the Victorian middle classes rated as only slightly less wicked than murder: she is a social climber who lies about her previously modest social status. The detective, at least in the sense that his suspicions propel the narrative, is Robert Audley, barrister and nephew of the elderly Sir Michael Audley, a man besotted by Lucy, who is neither what she appears or claims to be. The novel ends with Lucy, Lady Audley, now married to Sir Michael, dispatched to a mental institution, a seemingly appropriate penalty for someone who attempts to redraw the boundaries of class and status for her own advancement.

A woman crime novelist of the 19th or early 20th century would have faced several problems. Principally, the figure who drives the narrative forward and solves the mystery must be a man. Even if this ordinance is accepted it is clear, from Braddon's work, that subsidiary women characters must also conform to certain stereotypes. Lucy, Lady Audley, does not—cannot—make use of conventional routes to economic and social improvement. These, limited as they were, involved activities available only to men. She, being guileful and beautiful, resorted to sex.

Here is Holmes reflecting, for Watson, on a recently solved case ('The Disappearance of Lady Frances Fairfax'):

> One of the most dangerous classes in the world...is the drifting and friendless woman. She is the most harmless and often the most useful of mortals, but she is the inevitable inciter of crimes in others. She is helpless...She is a stray chicken in a world of foxes. When she is gobbled up she is hardly missed.

Holmes's image of womanhood seems to have little in common with Lady Audley, but mixed in with his condescending pity for the 'drifting and friendless woman' is a sense of unease, even distaste; a suspicion that she might prompt terrible things 'in others', specifically men, much as Braddon's character had charmed Sir Michael Audley.

The first female detective was the invention of a man. In Collins's *The Woman in White* (1860) Marian Halcombe, Laura Fairlie's devoted half-sister, is Walter Hartright's intellectual equal and plays an important role in solving the Byzantine mystery of the relationship between Laura and the spectral woman of the title. Walter's introduction of her to the reader is calculatedly unsettling. 'I said to myself, the lady is dark. She moved forward a few steps—and I said to myself, the lady is young. She approached nearer—and I said to myself with a sense of surprise which words fail me to express—the lady is ugly!' It is a masterpiece of timing and false expectation. In as much as contemporary writing allowed, Hartright is building into his accumulation of impressions a collateral sense of erotic anticipation. The question, which he never answers straightforwardly, is whether he finds her ugliness disappointing. Gradually, as the narrative continues, we begin to suspect that he is reassured by it. She is a woman, certainly, but she is made exempt from the complications of her gender. Men do not treat her as a potential partner or conquest and she is thus able to operate in an asexual vacuum.

Collins seems to anticipate Gilbert and Gubar's thesis that the novel provides special opportunities for women authors and characters, and he adds a coda: the role of the detective presupposes notions of authority and independence that are quintessentially male; women detectives must therefore eschew certain aspects of femininity, in Halcombe's case physical attractiveness.

Amelia Butterworth was introduced by Anna Katherine Green in *That Affair Next Door* (1897). She is treated as the prototype for the so-called 'spinster sleuth' mainly because Christie acknowledged Green and Butterworth as the inspiration for Miss Marple. She was preceded, just, by Loveday Brooke in Catherine L. Pirkis's collection *The Experiences of Loveday Brooke, Lady Detective* (1894) and followed shortly afterwards by Grant Allen's Lois Cayley in *Miss Cayley's Adventures* (1899). Butterworth is far duller than the rest and her abilities are only evident because she finds herself assisting the intellectually moribund New York police officer Ebenezer Gryce. All of these women have key elements in common, however. None displays characteristics that would at the time be associated with womanhood. Men rarely, if ever, are attracted to them, a curiosity that none of their authors, unlike Collins, takes the trouble to explain, and even on the rare occasion that a husband and family exist (see George R. Sims's *Dorcas Dene, Detective*, 1897) they are shuffled well into the background. A notable exception is Kate Goelet, an attractive, intelligent New York detective. Her career is brief because when a fellow sleuth courts and eventually marries her she gives up her profession (see *The Lady Detective*, 1890, by Harlan P. Halsey). The message appears to be that detection and the expectations of womanhood, at least as the latter were perceived at the time, are incompatible.

In the relatively few novels featuring a woman detective produced between the period of Holmes and the Golden Age the unaffiliated spinster prevailed. Tish Carberry, featured first in *The Amazing Adventures of Letitia Carberry* (1911), continued to appear in short stories until 1937, and her author Mary Roberts Rinehart also invented the nurse-detective Hilda Adams. The title of one of the novels involving the latter, *Miss Pinkerton* (1932), is indicative of Rinehart's technique. Her characters are, at least as professional stereotypes, asexual: women who elect not to act as women in order to take on roles routinely allocated to men. Carberry and Adams might, for all we know, harbour feelings about specific male characters, about family and children, or their perception of themselves as outsiders in a patriarchal domain, but we can only speculate on such matters because they never disclose such feelings, even privately to the reader. This theme is maintained in Hugh C. Weir's *Miss Madelyn Meek, Detective* (1914), a ludicrous female-American version of Holmes. Meek is more socially acceptable than Doyle's creation. She is reclusive but she finds solace in Coca Cola rather than cocaine. Her English counterpart is Baroness Emmuska Orczy's *Lady Molly of Scotland Yard* (1910). It is difficult to decide on whether Orczy is caricaturing her own class, the aristocracy, or if she and Lady Molly have unwittingly become part of a farce. The Watson role of worthy retainer and narrator is filled by her former maid Mary Granard, who is brighter than we might expect of a servant but still Lady Molly's adulatory inferior. We begin to suspect that Orczy herself takes all of this seriously only when it becomes clear that Molly's long-term motive is to free her wrongfully convicted husband from imprisonment. At that point the mood becomes sombre and having fulfilled her wifely duties Lady Molly retires from her role as head of the 'Female Department' at Scotland Yard, implying that women of a certain calibre are as a rule not disposed to such vulgar, grisly activities.

Golden Age singletons

Clearly the spinster detectives of the Golden Age are scions of the retiring and sometimes sequestered women of turn-of-the-century crime fiction. Christie's Jane Marple could be Amelia Butterworth reborn in the English home counties of the 1930s (Figure 4). Butterworth was pressurized by inauspicious circumstances, particularly the threatening, potentially violent atmosphere of New York and a police force made up exclusively of men. Marple is too old to be treated as a woman capable of provoking the baser instincts of males; she is content with such pastimes as knitting, gardening, and bird-watching and as a consequence is able to operate without causing anyone to suspect she is alert to their activities and motives. As a device in the puzzle–solution structure of traditional crime writing, Miss Marple is very effective, yet at the same time we cannot ignore the fact that she earns her status at the expense of women as a whole. True, she is possessed of formidable intelligence and moral fortitude, but she must trade presence for invisibility to exercise her convictions.

Miss Marple could be related to Patricia Wentworth's Miss Maud Silver, an ageing spinster who pursued her surrogate career as a private investigator from *Grey Mask* (1928) to *The Girl in the Cellar* (1961). Silver too enjoys knitting and spends her time, in mysteriously wealthy retirement as an ex-governess, solving crimes. More daring is Mrs (Dame) Beatrice Adela Lestrange Bradley, a Freudian who employs her skills as a professional psychoanalyst to analyse crimes and misdemeanours. She is not an elderly spinster but her status as a widow with no apparent wish to find another male partner seems by implication to be her licence to independence. Her creator, Gladys Mitchell, appears to be casting a mischievous glance towards the Marple stereotype because Bradley is an engaging compendium of gender contradictions. Married at least twice, she appears emotionally indifferent to her past, including the children from her relationships,

4. Margaret Rutherford playing Agatha Christie's Miss Marple. 'Was she a feminist icon who carved out an independent way for herself?' (*The Lady*, 2013)

and capable of striking fear into everyone she encounters, male or female. She is referred to as 'Mrs Crocodile' and aside from her intellectual strengths is renowned for her unfeminine physical power, on one occasion bringing her fist to a man's chest 'like an iron bolt'.

In 1929 Dorothy L. Sayers wrote in the Introduction to *The Omnibus of Crime Fiction* that most women detectives so far 'have not been very successful'. They have failed mainly because to be credible they are obliged to behave like women, favouring an 'irritatingly intuitive' approach above 'the logical' and being hampered by such diversions as marriage. One has to wonder if Mitchell's creation (who first appeared in *The Saltmarsh Murders*, 1932) was a response to this defeatist assessment. Sayers was at the time working on *Strong Poison* (1930) in which Lord Peter Wimsey meets Harriet Vane. The latter has studied at Oxford, writes crime novels, and dabbles in real-life detection. She is also the first 'spinster sleuth' with a sex life, or at least the first on record. In fact Wimsey is responsible for securing her acquittal on a charge of murdering her lover. In *Gaudy Night* (1935) we begin to wonder if Sayers is toying with a curious hybrid; something that is ostensibly a crime novel but which enables her also to explore the question of gender equality, at least so far as such things could be countenanced by the English middle classes of the 1930s. Wimsey allows, indeed encourages, Harriet to risk her life during the investigation, stating later that he has now 'cleared all scores', having previously saved her from execution. They achieve a degree of emotional and intellectual equality but Sayers goes on to question the validity of her own undertaking. In an otherwise gratuitous subtext Wimsey offers Harriet advice on how to rescue Wilfred, a fictional character in her own ongoing novel, from being little more than 'the world's worst goop'. He suggests that she tells the reader something of Wilfred's troubled background, which will counterbalance his outward impressions with psychological depth. She decides against this because such complexities are, she feels, ill-suited to the nature of detective fiction which is more a form of entertainment than an engagement with the actual turmoils of existence. One can't help but notice the parallels between Wilfred and Wimsey and more significantly between Harriet's sense of the limitations of the crime genre and Sayers's attempt to overreach them. It seems both odd and unfair that Gladys Mitchell's reputation is so completely eclipsed by that of Sayers.

Reactions to masculinity

Across the Atlantic, Chandler in his manifesto for hard-boiled/ noir writing, 'The Simple Art of Murder', made it clear that the predominant figure in any novel which dared to depict American society at its worst could only be male. There are no women detectives in the subgenre dominated by Chandler, Hammett, and Cain. Instead male characters, investigators and villains alike, are obliged to deal more with erotic force-fields than human beings. In *Double Indemnity* Cain comes close to causing us to sympathize with Huff who, despite himself, commits murder because of the twin attractions of Phyllis and her equally sensual stepdaughter Lola.

Chandler's least conventional treatment of gender is in *The Lady in the Lake* (1943) in which both the reader and Marlowe lose track of a narrative that page-by-page becomes increasingly complex and indecipherable. Adultery, theft, fraud, and murder all feature but nothing is ever quite as it appears even when facts are disclosed. The figure who choreographs this *danse macabre* is Mildred Haviland who deceives or seduces all of the principal male characters and creates an even more perplexing gallery of deceptions for the women by variously disguising herself as them or murdering them. She is eventually found naked and dead in the lake but Chandler never pretends to understand her in terms of what she is really like as an individual or what motivates her. Like Phyllis and many other temptresses in the noir books, Mildred exploits her own sexuality; but she goes further than that. By evading Marlowe as an individual she displaces him as Chandler's instrument of narrative control. She forces her author to write a book about something that neither he nor his fictional representative can claim to comprehend. The novel engages with issues of gender decades before the rise of feminism as a literary and cultural force and it does so by raising questions about representation that continue to trouble us.

Almost two generations after *Gaudy Night*, Harriet Vane returned as P. D. James's Cordelia Gray in *An Unsuitable Job For a Woman* (1972). James seems determined to obstruct her attempts to become a private investigator. She is 22 years old (while Vane was 30) and her apparent immaturity seems to cement the belief among the men she has to deal with that she is indeed 'unsuitable' for the job she craves. But against these odds she succeeds and critics are still puzzled by James's presentation of her a decade later in *The Skull Beneath the Skin* (1982). In this book she is vulnerable, plagued by doubts about her own abilities, and prone to making recklessly misguided errors. Between the two novels feminism had become a more powerful and vocal presence in society and literature. Was James, through Gray, asserting her conservatism or was she, like Sayers half a century before, declaring that crime writing was not a proper forum for such elemental debates as gender equality?

From the late 1970s onwards the legacy of the hard-boiled tradition of crime writing exercised either a direct or a pernicious influence on women novelists. In Britain writers such as Ruth Rendell and Susan Hill created male detectives who seemed designed to counterbalance the aggressive masculinity of Chandler's 'mean streets' figures. Rendell's long-running (1964–2013) Detective Chief Inspector Wexford exhibits poise even when faced with the most appalling crimes and shows an exemplary concern for relatives of the victims. He resembles a cross between one's favourite uncle and a trauma counsellor, the complete antithesis of hyperactive wise-cracking anti-heroes sustained in the work of Ed McBain, Micky Spillane, and Ross Macdonald. Hill's Detective Inspector Simon Serrailler is possessed of a sensibility so delicate as to make Dalgleish seem coarse, even rakish, by comparison.

The Thatcher decade inspired a number of British women writers to make use of crime fiction partly as a means of commenting on the transitions and undercurrents of society and also as a vehicle for woman characters, detectives and narrators, as feminist presences. Gillian Slovo's five detective novels featuring Kate Baeier began with *Morbid Symptoms* (1984). Each is narrated by Baeier, who struggles to make a living as a private eye and follows a second career as investigative journalist. This allows her to take a step back from the male-orientated world of crime, private-detection, and police work and it is clear that Slovo is at once undermining and exploiting the standard conventions of the genre. Baeier often echoes the wry cynical mode of Marlowe but while Chandler's creation is unpersuaded by anything resembling abstract ideals, Slovo allows Baeier to function as a prism for left-wing, feminist principles. The novels are, at least in spirit, autobiographical; both of Slovo's parents were anti-Apartheid activists and her mother was murdered by South African agents. She moved to London aged 12 and Baeier was a response to the right-wing agenda of the Thatcher government and its policy of appeasement regarding South Africa. Does crime writing suit Slovo's polemical objective? Baeier is certainly not presented as an untarnished agent of probity nor does she offer clumsy ideological explanations for every kind of misdemeanour, but she is alert to questions about why people can treat each other so foully; her particular branch of the genre might be called 'enlightened noir'.

Rebecca O'Rourke in her debut novel *Jumping the Cracks* (1987) introduces the first genuinely working-class woman detective. Rats is from Yorkshire, a lesbian who left school without much of an education and eschewed the hard-won erudition of the autodidact; she prefers *The Daily Mirror* and TV. She therefore challenges both of the prevailing stereotypes of detective fiction: the intellectual who disentangles the complexities of the mystery and the predominantly male non-conformist who relies on a combination of guile and violence. The plot reflects Rats's haphazard life-style in that she discovers the body of a murder victim and despite her better instincts tries to make sense of what happened, without any clear sense of duty or moral purpose. Improbably she uncovers enough detail to disclose the identity of the perpetrator, a man who exists in a different zone of existence, involving high finance and political power. She sends a file on him to the police and retires back into the faintly anarchic world of the urban dispossessed. The novel is original but by equal degrees improbable and, some might say, sanctimonious. Even if we suspend disbelief sufficiently to take Rats seriously, the world of villains she confronts has a rather simplistic air of pure evil about it. The villain, for example, is called Cruse Pershing.

A few years earlier, the American author Marcia Muller launched a series of novels involving Sharon McCone, beginning with *Edwin of the Iron Shoes* (1977). McCone conducts sexual relationships with men on her own terms, displaying sufficient emotion to show she is responsive to the feelings of others but not enough to render her vulnerable to unnecessary commitments. She dresses and behaves in a way that can be classified as feminine while taking pride in her ability with firearms and her adeptness in violent physical confrontations. One begins to suspect that a formula is being applied, in that Muller appears determined to at once override, without replicating, the predominantly masculine features of the quintessential hard-boiled detective. Readers can judge her abilities for themselves, but it must be said that in her use of style as a challenge to her male predecessors (she sometimes reads like a clumsy amalgam of Hammett and Spillane) she is often the self-evident loser: frequently the effort involved in the performance is a little too tangible. However, the three most popular women crime fiction authors of recent decades ground their writings in similar hypothetical challenges. Sara Paretsky, Sue Grafton, and Patricia Cornwell, and their detectives—respectively V. I. Warshawski, Kinsey Millhone, and Kay Scarpetta—tell us a great deal about how notions of vehement masculinity have become so deeply embedded in the legacy of crime fiction, especially that branch of the genre which lays a claim towards realism. Each embodies a very pragmatic utilitarian brand of feminism in that they have little time for all-encompassing ideological theses but are committed to, and proud of, the doctrine of self-determination. They succeed, despite their generally blue-collar backgrounds, and the challenges that women inevitably face in a world involving criminality and, in Scarpetta's case, police-procedure pathology.

Grafton's Millhone is given to reflect, via her narrator, on the ways in which conventional expectations of womanhood can be telescoped into ambitions and a sense of independence that transcend such stereotypes. She is grateful to her eccentric aunt:

> Firing a handgun, she felt, would teach me to appreciate both safety and accuracy. It would also help me develop good hand–eye co-ordination, which she thought was useful. She'd taught me to knit and crochet so that I'd learn patience and an eye for detail.
>
> (*D is For Deadbeat*, p. 102)

It is difficult to imagine Sam Spade conceding that his handgun skills in some way relate to his childhood instructions in crocheting but in another respect the two characters beg comparison; for each, irony guarantees an absence of conceitedness.

Millhone, Warshawski, and Scarpetta—like Sharon McCone—step cautiously between conventionally prescribed gender roles. Each has a relationship with a man, or men, but they impose strict limitations on themselves. Millhone:

> A woman should never, never, be financially dependent on anyone, especially a man, because the minute you were dependent, you could be abused.
>
> (*D is For Deadbeat*, p. 102)

Warshawski, following her mother's death, commits herself to exemption from commitment, be this emotional or financial.

> I knew then that it was a terrible mistake to depend on someone else to solve my problems for me. Now I seem to be too terrorised to

solve them for myself and I'm thrashing around. But when I ask for
help it just drives me wild.

(Toxic Shock, p. 221)

Warshawski is certainly too complex and multi-dimensional to be
regarded as an instrument for gender equality yet she must also
be seen as reflecting a culture that has moved beyond the seemingly
intractable models of the detective created by Cain, Hammett,
Chandler, et al. Like her male predecessors she is something of a
fantasy—reckless daredevils who solve mysteries that leave the
police dumbfounded are the stuff of escapism—yet as an individual
she is beguiling. When in *Toxic Shock* she decides to act as a
vigilante and shoots dead the manager of a poison-spreading
chemical plant, we forget that this is standard crime fiction. She
tells us, first person, how she feels about killing a man and suddenly
we are in the territory of Dostoevsky; existential torment supplants
the thrill of investigation. And when Warshawski returns us
yet again to her emotional attachment with her mother, and her
uncertain feelings about preparing for her lover Morrell's return from
Afghanistan, we are struck by Paretsky's achievement in creating a
character to whom we respond at so many different emotional levels.
Warshawski's presence at the vortex of a conventional mystery
drives the narrative forward but we are just as engaged with the
mysterious convergences of past and present that constitute her
personality. Can this be said of Spade or Chandler, individuals
who entertain us but deflect questions regarding what they are
really like with an elegantly robust carapace of style?

The issues of gender-difference and sexuality raise intriguing
questions about the somewhat predictable, even monolithic,
character of conventional crime fiction because alongside those
women writers who have regularly produced bestsellers and
earned themselves the status of literary celebrities there is an
extraordinary number of lesser-known novelists, albeit mostly
Americans, who have elected to harness the genre to seemingly

incongruous themes. The mid-1980s, for example, saw a boom in novels featuring lesbian detectives: Katherine V. Forrest, Nikki Baker, Lauren Wright Douglas, Claire McNab, Barbara Wilson, and Vicki P. McConnell are notable among these authors. Wilson exemplifies key aspects of this trend by creating persistent tensions between what virtually all readers would recognize as the components of a crime fiction plot (misdemeanour, clues, suspects, motive, investigator, etc.) and features of the text that work against any notion of an explanation or a solution; see particularly her *Sisters of the Road* (1986). The implication seems to be that restoring order, ensuring that the aberrant conforms to a securely perceptible routine, is an endemic feature of societies still founded upon patriarchal ideology and that even those women detectives who claim a degree of self determination are in truth mimicking their male counterparts. Irrespective of one's opinion on the socio-political import of such works one is struck by how the very notion of the crime genre—involving as it does an abstention from the responsibilities of 'literary' novels—presents such a challenge to writers who are as much activists as entertainers. In this regard black women investigators appear equally magnetized by the seemingly inhospitable legacy of detective fiction. Not all of the novelists are women of colour but the prospect of experimenting with the unsteady cocktail of gender, race, policing, and the judiciary has inspired such post-1980s novelists as Valerie Wilson Wesley, Eleanor Taylor Bland, Grace Edwards, and Barbara Neely. Particularly impressive is Neely's amateur detective Blanche White (see *Blanche on the Lam*, 1992) who is black and a domestic servant. Blanche has a significant advantage over other fictional investigators in that to virtually everyone else she is invisible. Because of her race, class, and gender no one notices her as she pursues her enquiries. Once more, a genre that emerged as an essentially male-orientated, white, middle-class form of entertainment proves an unusual means of exposing the in-built prejudices of society.

Chapter 6
Spy fiction, the thriller and legal drama

Espionage

When we open a crime novel we enter a world which is both addictive yet manifestly unreal and in this respect the genre has much in common with spy fiction. Both are concerned with covert activity that for the duration of the book is compelling, convincing, and manifestly unreal. Until recently the UK denied that the secret services existed. Even now, when MI5 and MI6 are acknowledged as actual organizations with particular histories and personnel, their day-to-day activities and the numerous projects that have featured in their respective histories are protected by the Official Secrets Act. Other countries, such as the US, which have been more frank about the existence of state-sponsored espionage and security agencies, have been similarly protective regarding their actions, procedures, and, most significantly, their possible licence to act outside the law. So while there are significant parallels between crime writing and spy fiction the latter can make a special claim to uniqueness: it is based on an activity about which we know very little.

The first espionage novel was James Fenimore Cooper's *The Spy* (1821), which charts the activities of one Harvey Birch during the war between the newly independent states of America and Britain. Birch disguises himself as a pedlar in order to travel covertly across battle lines, collecting information on British tactics and deployments and delivering this to his American comrades. Cooper implies that Birch is based on fact, albeit unrecorded, that he is one of many Americans who 'wore masks'—i.e. assumed disguises—to serve the interests of their country. There are detailed references to particular points in Westchester County where battles occurred and as a final attempt at authenticity Cooper depicts a meeting between Birch and George Washington, in which the latter assures Birch that he has served his nation with honour and courage.

The fact that Birch and his undercover confederates were largely freelance, inspired by patriotic idealism but without being accountable to anything resembling an organized unit, was probably the reason why the novel was followed by nothing remotely similar for almost a century. Espionage might have been undertaken by individuals but espionage agencies did not exist until the beginning of the 20th century, when factional hostility and colonial envy were fomenting the tensions in Europe that would eventually lead to the outbreak of World War I in 1914.

William Le Queux fed feelings of uncertainty verging on panic in Britain by juxtaposing the steady complacencies of society as experienced by most of his readers with a sense of nervous subterfuge. Novels such as *The Invasion of 1910* (1906) predicted that Germany had already begun to implement plans for a seaborne invasion of Britain by placing spies at all levels of society who were regularly sending back reports on military and civil targets. His *Spies of the Kaiser* (1909) presented a scenario of infiltration by German espionage agents so convincing that it is now recognized by historians of the secret service as instrumental in the formation of MI5, the internal security agency, during the year of its publication. Le Queux's work was sensationalist and xenophobic, and *The Spies of the Kaiser* sold four million copies during the years before the war. His inspiration was a far more subtle and challenging novel, Erskine Childers's *The Riddle of the Sands* (1903). This involves a narrative by Carruthers, a Foreign Office civil servant, which Childers edits as if it were an authentic memoir. Carruthers has been summoned by his friend Davies to join him on a yachting expedition around the coast of Frisia and Davies tells of how he has recently encountered a Captain Dollmann who he believes is involved in plans to mount a German invasion from the Frisian coast. Carruthers, with the assistance of Childers, presents himself as a potentially unreliable witness, symptomatic of a growing nationwide neurosis about the motives of other European powers, Germany in particular, and we remain uncertain as to the validity or otherwise of Davies's fears until the end of the novel.

The plots focus upon individuals, figures who might be disguising their true affiliations and conspiring against those they have deceived. They are personifications of a general feeling of anxiety that came from there having been no significant military conflicts in Europe since the Napoleonic wars of a century earlier. It was feared that pressures for the outbreak of such conflicts were building and the image of individuals who might be part of some horrible conspiracy fed upon these agitations. Even in Rudyard Kipling's *Kim* (1901), the eponymous boy, abroad in the Indian subcontinent, becomes a metaphor for the need for action against those who might threaten the Empire. Kim teaches himself subterfuge because it is clear that others are better practised in such dark arts, Russians in particular.

Walter Wood's *The Enemy in Our Midst* (1906) is more melodramatic and preposterous than anything by Le Queux, with German immigrants presented as so numerous and devious as to be on the point of taking over London, without the assistance of military intervention. Joseph Conrad, aware of the state of panic that inspired and sustained this new brand of fiction, produced *The Secret Agent* (1907). The novel is set in the 1880s when Britain was experiencing its first bout of mass hysteria, this time based on a growing conviction that London, like other European capitals, was alive with murderous, sometimes suicidal, groups of anarchists. In 1884 an anarchist had blown himself to pieces during an attempt to place a bomb in the Greenwich Observatory. The Agent of Conrad's title, Adolf Verloc, leads a double life as a member of an anarchist group and as an informer on the London Embassy of an unspecified European state. He also owns a shop in Soho that deals in bric-a-brac and, more profitably, contraceptive devices and pornography. This hint at a seedier aspect of subterfuge provides Conrad with a lead-in to the prevailing temper of the novel. As an aesthetic movement Surrealism was in its infancy but the figures who make up *The Secret Agent* are sufficiently unhinged and grotesque to recommend themselves as its first fictional manifestations in English. Conrad's objective was to ridicule and defuse the ongoing preoccupation with bands of subversives at work throughout British society, and a year later G. K. Chesterton in *The Man Who Was Thursday* (1908) followed suit. There is no evidence that Chesterton's novel was inspired by Conrad's—in practical terms this was impossible given that the two books were completed within months of each other—but they are extraordinarily similar, with Gregory Syme recruited to an anarchist group while working as an informer for Scotland Yard. It gradually becomes evident that all members of the group are government spies, reporting back to various police bodies on the activities of their apparent comrades. The subversives do not actually exist and, in Chesterton's view, the sense of threat experienced by everyone at the time was a case of paranoid self-delusion.

Nonetheless, John Buchan's immensely successful *The Thirty-Nine Steps* (1915), published a year after war was declared and based on the fictional Richard Hannay's pursuit of a network of German agents in Scotland, could claim a secure grounding in fact. In October 1914 Carl Hans Lody was arrested and evidence later presented at his trial showed that he had been working undercover in Edinburgh and sending messages on British naval operations in the Firth of Forth which resulted in the torpedoing of HMS *Pathfinder* by a U-boat.

W. Somerset Maugham was the first to produce crime novels based on his personal experience of espionage. He had worked for MI6 in Switzerland and Russia during World War I but in translating facts into fiction he faced the dilemma of having to pretend that the former were entirely inauthentic: to have done otherwise would have caused him to breach the Official Secrets Act. As a consequence the eponymous anti-hero of *Ashenden or, The British Agent* (1928) appears to spend his time dealing with routine and inconsequential matters. Maugham set out to deglamorize espionage, causing it to become both believable and unremarkable. Similarly Graham Greene, who had also worked part-time for MI6, created, in pieces such as *The Confidential Agent* (1939) and *Our Man In Havana* (1958), the image of the spy as the unacknowledged, sometimes farcical, foot soldier of global political conflicts.

Since the 1960s one novelist has dominated British spy fiction and his importance and qualities as a writer per se have been obscured by the down-market, populist reputation of his chosen genre. John le Carré's best-known work is the trilogy of novels featuring the MI6 agent George Smiley, *Tinker, Tailor, Soldier, Spy* (1974), *The Honourable Schoolboy* (1977), and *Smiley's People* (1979). Smiley is an idealist wrapped in an enigma. Half the time he puts up with life as a reclusive scholarly figure, regularly cuckolded by his aristocrat wife and disobliged by ambitious, purblind colleagues. When yoked into action he embodies the best one would expect of the Western democratic conscience. He is a sceptic, distrusting of all abstract systems of ideology, but he has an instinctive, empowering recognition of the basic distinctions between right and wrong. The engine of the trilogy is the long-term conflict between Smiley and the quasi-monastic KGB figure Karla. The various strategies and responses engineered by each propel narratives that offer some of the most challenging questions in fiction regarding the nature and ethics of the Cold War. Le Carré offers the prose equivalent of epic poems in which the absolutes of existence are lain bare and scrutinized, and here we face a paradox. No other novelist can claim to have written so challengingly and with such authority about the nature of the post-World War II global enmity between Western democracy and the Soviet bloc, but because le Carré's work is designated as a non-mainstream subgenre, an entertainment, his achievement has gone largely unrecognized.

As the polarities of the Cold War gradually mutated into localized conflicts so le Carré began to turn his attention to what had been at the peripheries of his 1960s and 1970s writing. In *The Secret Pilgrim* (1991) Smiley reflects upon how the West had maintained its conscience because of, not despite, the threatening presence of the post-Stalin monolith, and in *A Perfect Spy* (1986) we witness via the suicidal Magnus Pym the destructive psychological effects of working in the intelligence community. In *The Little Drummer Girl* (1983) an English actress is recruited by Israeli intelligence to infiltrate a Palestinian terrorist network and this theme of the somewhat listless individual suddenly obliged to confront moral and political issues as participant rather than an opinionated outsider became the predominant theme of most of his novels of the 1990s and 2000s: *The Russia House* (1989) shows us the disintegrating Soviet Union and *Single and Single* (1999) explores the effects of this upon the disputed territories of the Caucasus. In *Absolute Friends* (2003) we follow Ted Mundy from his childhood in post-imperial Pakistan, through the riot-torn West Berlin of the late 1960s and Cold War espionage to the present day of obsessive counterterrorism. *The Constant Gardener* (2001) is le Carré's exploration of the hypocrisies and hidden motives that underpin the industrialized world's patronage of poverty-stricken Africa. He once told an interviewer that 'the spy novel encapsulated ... public wariness about political behaviour and about the set-up, the fix of society' (*Newsagent and Bookseller*). In the modern world where political strategies and their consequences are filtered through a bewildering network of discourses—some costive and protective, others provocatively misleading—the spy, even the involuntary type, becomes a special kind of witness, able uniquely to experience the divergence of truth from public dissimulation.

Le Carré can make a particular claim upon uniqueness since none of his competitors comes close to his achievement of transforming the spy novel from a self-limiting subgenre to a chronicle which surpasses mainstream fiction in its capacity to deal with world issues. Len Deighton, first with Harry Palmer (*The Ipcress File*, 1962; *Funeral in Berlin*, 1964) and later Bernard Sampson ('Game, Set and Match' trilogy, 1983–5; 'Hook, Line and Sinker' trilogy 1988–90), deglamorized intelligence work and extended the Greene tradition of grimy authenticity but in the end his novels reflect little more than a self-consuming inward-looking state of mind. More recently, Alan Judd has produced retrospective novels focusing upon the role of MI6 during the Cold War (see *Legacy*, 2001) yet despite his qualities as a writer and historian he only tackles issues that le Carré had explored and left behind with Smiley.

Henry Porter in *Remembrance Day* (1999), *A Spy's Life* (2001), and *Empire State* (2003) attempts with Robert Harland to amalgamate the repressed, quietly tortured Englishness of Smiley with a more glamorous international lifestyle and narrative. In the end the latter triumphs, and excitement is substituted for le Carré's meticulous pathology of an era and a dilemma.

Many novels, including those that do not even hint at criminality, could be said to 'thrill' us in the sense that we become apprehensive about, often excited by, the fate of skilfully delineated characters. But the more popular version of thriller writing is characterized by the exaggeration of acts and characteristics that enable the reader to exchange anything resembling credulity for fantasy and escapism. Sensation novels are treated as ancestors to classic detective fiction, yet one could just as easily regard the quasi-Gothic air of falsehood that informs many of them as prerequisites for the modern thriller. Equally, a number of the 'noir' writers who began to publish in *Black Mask* went on to produce novels which sated their readers' appetites for a combination of violence and eroticism, irrespective of the question of who committed a particular crime. I would regard such works as hybrids, exploring still uncharted territories beyond the continuously evolving mainstream of crime writing. The first writer to chart a properly independent course towards the thriller as a brand of writing independent from mainstream crime and spy fiction was Ian Fleming. In *From Russia With Love* (1957) we are treated to a description of the instruments of death, including 'a flat throwing knife, built by Wilkinson's, the sword makers' and the silencer for a Beretta hidden in a tub of Palmolive shaving cream. The showy abundance of weaponry is accompanied by references to the exceptional standard and cost of camouflage, including the hirsute leather of the case. In the opening chapters of *Moonraker* (1955) we are allowed access to clubs, particularly their dining rooms, which seem exempt from the deprivations of rationing that had been lifted a year before its publication. Bond lives in a different world from that of even his wealthier readers, a world that also involves epic fights to the death with agencies of evil and encounters with beautiful women. Fleming worked for the intelligence services but his fictional account of spying was pure invention. It is instructive to compare Bond's encounters with M, one of which occurs adjacent to a 'cold table, laden with lobsters, pies, joints and delicacies in aspic', with Alec Leamas's meetings with Control, his MI6 boss, in le Carré's *The Spy Who Came In From the Cold* (1963), a novel which carries an air of grubby austerity.

> Leamas sat down in a chair facing an olive green electric fire with a bowl of water balanced on top of it.
>
> 'Do you find it cold?' Control asked. He was stooping over the fire rubbing his hands together. He wore a cardigan under his black jacket, a shabby brown one. (p. 17)

Even if a reader believed that espionage actually occurred, they would not envy Leamas's unglamorous, often humiliating experiences. Bond, conversely, is the cynosure of every male fantasy.

Escapism and the thriller

Eric Ambler was a near contemporary of Fleming and although their work seems to differ greatly, Ambler's prevailing theme of the 'innocent abroad' indicates their shared characteristics as thriller writers. In *The Mask of Demetrios* (1939) and twenty years later in *Passage of Arms* (1959) ordinary people—respectively the academic Charles Latimer and an American couple, the Nilsens—are drawn into unwarranted encounters with agents of global conflict. The novels use these figures as avatars for the same desire for escapism that ensured the popularity of Bond. Certainly, neither Latimer nor the Nilsens become willingly involved in intercontinental arms trading or sinister communist conspiracies, but their transition from the routine to the unaccountable and the exotic mirrors the transformative power of the thriller as a genre. Unlike other derivatives of mainstream crime writing it exchanges virtually all notions of credibility for access to the otherwise inconceivable.

The most enduring model for this brand of escapist thriller pits the state or even larger global power structures against robust, sometimes absurdly fantastic, notions of individuality. Frederick Forsyth's *The Day of the Jackal* (1971) fed upon rumours of how right-wing politicians, with military backing, were hatching plots against democratically elected governments in the West which were thought weak in the face of the increasing influence of revolutionary socialism. It tells the story, based partly on fact, of how French paramilitaries had hired a professional assassin to kill President Charles de Gaulle. We are gripped by the meticulous and gradual increase in tension, eventually convincing us that the unnamed hit man might well succeed, and also by our divided affiliations. Rationally we want him to be caught before he shoots de Gaulle, yet at the same time we are mesmerized by the assassin's convincing ingenuity and, though we shouldn't be, impressed by his ability to keep one step ahead of Interpol, the French police, and security services.

Gerald Seymour, like Forsyth a television journalist, was impressed by the popularity of *The Day of the Jackal* and followed it with a similar formula in *Harry's Game* (1975). This time the assassination of a British Cabinet Minister by an IRA terrorist is successful and an undercover army officer is dispatched to track down the killer. Seymour went on to base novels on some aspects of the Cold War, the Arab–Israeli conflict, Iranian conspiracies against the West, and the Anti-Apartheid Movement. Throughout we find that the theme of singularity—admirable or repulsive—is given greater emphasis by the power and inflexibility of whatever opposes it.

Craig Thomas's *Firefox* (1977) updates the technological wizardry of the Bond novels, with the invention of an impressive accumulation of stealth technology, in this case a MiG fighter capable of five times the speed of sound and a weapons system activated by the thought impulses of the pilot. Mitchell Gant, a US Vietnam veteran pilot, is dispatched to the USSR to steal the plane. Every aspect of the book is absurdly improbable but, assisted by a film version directed by and starring Clint Eastwood as Gant, it became a bestseller.

The Cold War inspired a good deal of thriller writers but any inclination to treat their books as a serious engagement with the possibility of global conflict should be tempered by what happened after the dissolution of the Soviet bloc in the early 1990s. An intriguing test case is the author Tom Clancy whose career spanned this extraordinary period of transition. His first novel *The Hunt for Red October* (1984) sold more than two million copies and it tells of how the CIA analyst Jack Ryan assists Captain Remius, disillusioned commander of the Soviet submarine of the title, to defect and to hand over his vessel to the US navy. After numerous rejections the book was eventually published by the Naval Institute Press who saw its potential as an instrument for propaganda, particularly during Ronald Reagan's promotion of even more sophisticated nuclear weapons systems. Reagan himself publicly praised the novel as 'my kind of yarn'.

Ryan presided as the principal figure in many of Clancy's later novels, and after the Communist bloc had ceased to pose a threat against free-market democracies in the real world even Ryan's more devoted fans must have begun to detect something ludicrous about his fictional escapades. In *Debt of Honor* (1994), for example, Japan is taken over by extremist nationalists, acquires nuclear weapons, and declares war on the US. The fate of the nation depends once more on Ryan's courage and ingenuity, especially since he is now President. From the early 1990s onwards Clancy, and Ryan, became book-by-book ever more desperate to find a sufficiently nasty substitute for the now departed evil empire of the Soviet Union.

A more prudent representation of Cold War anxiety was Martin Cruz Smith's *Gorky Park* (1981). Arkady Renko, investigating detective in the Moscow Militsiya, is as sceptical as Clancy's Remius about the benefits of the Soviet State, but after a brief visit to the US a mixture of weary nostalgia and love draws him back to his dysfunctional homeland. Like Ryan, Renko survives in Smith's fiction for three decades and similarly one begins to discern something close to desperation in his later novels—sometimes based in Putin's Russia and on one occasion in Cuba: a search for something as satisfyingly inflexible as the old Soviet monolith against which he can test his own feelings of hopelessness.

Eric Ludlum's trilogy of novels following the exploits of renegade-amnesiac CIA agent Jason Bourne (1980, 1986, 1990) deals obliquely with the Soviet Union as a threat to Europe and the US, but Bourne's glowering presence is almost reassuring, at least compared with the Byzantine web of conspiracies against which he has to contend. After 1991, Ludlum's books, and his heroes, follow Clancy's into a search for something to replace the old enemy. In *The Apocalypse Watch* (1995) agent Drew Latham takes on single-handedly a web of neo-Nazis who have infiltrated virtually every level of government in Europe and the US. There are some instances in which the suspension of disbelief involves a painful and Herculean effort.

There have, of course, been numerous developments in global politics during the last three decades which give us cause to revise the thesis famously promoted by Francis Fukuyama that the close of the 1980s marked 'The End of History', not least the ongoing debate on the nature of climate change. In Michael Crichton's *State of Fear* (2004) a group of eco-campaigners adopt a policy of terrorism, including acts of mass murder, to draw attention to, as they see it, a state of imminent global catastrophe. The key figure in the narrative is the environmentalist lawyer Peter Evans who is ideologically sympathetic to the eco-terrorists' cause and burdened with the task of preventing them from engineering natural disasters.

Again, the formula of the individual struggling against a monolithic force predominates and Crichton himself in a personal afterword refers to the rumours that a 'politico-legal-media' complex had been formed during the 1990s to spread fear-inducing notions of imminent 'crisis' and apocalyptic 'disaster': mass trepidation as a means of social control. The terrifying prospect of nuclear war had been replaced by a carefully orchestrated fear of imminent ecological catastrophe. Crichton neither endorses nor dismisses this thesis, leaving it up to the reader to follow Peter Evans through a maze of unresolved questions.

For all its faults—particularly, as many scientists pointed out, his manipulation of proven facts—Crichton's book is a commendable dramatization of debates surrounding climate change, charging Evans, as the reader's representative, with enormous challenges and responsibilities. At the other end of the post-Cold War spectrum of courageous individualism we find Lee Child's Jack Reacher novels. In the 1950s Bond provided relief from the dreary monochrome world of many of his readers, but Fleming's brand of escapism is accompanied by a slight but discernible hint of self-caricature. Reacher is by equal degrees ludicrous and monotonously self-absorbed. He is able to resist all forms of violent assault, outstandingly beautiful women are magnetized by his presence (a charismatic gift that is not apparent to the reader), and his lifestyle is absurd—he wanders from one life-threatening adventure to the next without addressing the implied question of why exactly he exists or how his apparently heedless wanderings seem designed to further test his almost superhuman capacities.

We should not, however, treat thrillers as solely a route to wish-fulfilment. Some appeal to our more ghoulish tastes, exaggerating the less endearing features of noir/hard-boiled writing. William Faulkner's *Sanctuary* (1931) is frightening mostly because we cannot fix clearly upon its principal subject. Is it the deranged, impotent gunman and rapist Popeye, or his victim, the judge's daughter Temple Drake, who is raped, frequently assaulted and finally confined in a Memphis brothel? The shifting double-focus causes us to wonder if we should be disgusted or sympathetic and the more we question our proper response the more we are drawn into the grotesque moral vacuum of the novel. James Hadley Chase followed Faulkner's example in *No Orchids for Miss Blandish* (1939), involving once more a disturbingly intimate encounter with an impotent psychopath. David Goodis's fiction of the 1940s and 50s is equally dysfunctional. In *Dark Passage* (1946) Goodis seems determined to undermine the standard procedures of crime fiction. Vincent Perry, mistakenly convicted of murdering his wife, escapes from jail and becomes himself a murderer in an attempt to prove his innocence. The message of the novel, if such can be discerned, is that we are always prey to legal and circumstantial anarchy and injustice and that in the end there are no such things as moral or legislative certainty. Norman Bates, who found global fame in Hitchcock's film, was born in Robert Bloch's novel *Psycho* (1959) and we find within this emerging trend a persistent tendency to focus on something that most of us speculate upon without ever expecting, or wishing, to know: the mental state of a psychopathic criminal. Are such books explorations of psychological and existential torment of the kind exemplified by Franz Kafka or do they play upon such topics simply to offer the reader the voyeuristic 'thrill' of watching murderous lunatics while not condoning their activities? I would contend that the latter case is backed by the more convincing evidence. For one thing each book dwells emphatically upon the nature of violent acts, giving special attention to the gratuitous, even uncomprehending nature of cruelty.

Jim Thompson's novels of the 1950s and 60s epitomize this brand of writing, particularly his *The Killer Inside Me* (1952). Twenty-nine-year-old Deputy Sheriff Lou Ford embodies the informal trustworthiness of everyone's ideal small-town lawman, until we are gradually drawn into his secret world. The disclosures begin with his sadomasochistic relationship with Joyce, a local prostitute, inspired it seems by his recollection of sexually abusing an infant when in his teens. His brother confessed to the crime, served a prison sentence, and was killed working on a building site after his release. Lou's own career as a vengeful, sadistic murderer—including his killing of Joyce—is causally related to what happened to his brother, at least if we trust the narrator. But the narrator is Lou himself and we must continually ask ourselves if the spectacle of a deranged serial killer employing pseudo-logic to explain his acts is instructive or ghoulishly gratifying.

The writer who has over the past three decades done most to blur the line between crime writing and several other popular subgenres—notably the thriller, science-fiction, and the horror story—is Stephen King. King is a prolific and seemingly eclectic writer but each of his works incorporates a common, signature feature. His debut novel *Carrie* (1974) was regarded by many in the US as horribly prescient and symptomatic of what would eventually become regular events: massacres, often of peers, by High School-age perpetrators with troubled or dysfunctional backgrounds. The factor that disqualifies the book as diagnostic is the eponymous murderess's telekinetic powers. Even in *Misery* (1987), his most naturalistic piece, in which an author is kidnapped by his most obsessive fan, there are hints at forces abroad that cannot be properly accounted for via reason or empirical evidence. Crime and evil are his prevailing concerns but he never indulges an exclusively post-Enlightenment explanation for either. In this respect he is a postmodern throwback to that early relative of the Sensation novel, the Gothic; his popularity appears to be sustained by a combination of an enduring taste for something terrifying and gruesome and a renewed fascination with the supernatural.

Like King, Jeffrey Deaver is a writer who has tapped into what appears be a nostalgic, even masochistic, desire for something beyond what the civilized world can accept or understand; but the best-known fictional psychopath of recent decades is Thomas Harris's Hannibal Lecter, who first appeared in *Red Dragon* (1981) and *The Silence of the Lambs* (1989). From the beginning Harris poses a question that will ensure the longevity of Lecter. Can we respond with anything other than horror to an erudite cosmopolitan who enjoys eating his victims? Without showing a hint of remorse for his activities Lecter attempts to cultivate alliances with members of the FBI, particularly Clarice Starling in the second book. In the early novels Starling treats his cooperative gestures with suspicion, verging on contempt, and in this respect she is the reader's surrogate, examining the relationship between repugnance and expedient indulgence from inside the narrative. Matters become even more complex in *Hannibal* (1999) where we learn of Hannibal's aristocratic lineage and that during the war his beloved younger sister Mischa was eaten by a gang of Wehrmacht deserters; the consequences for Lecter's taste for human flesh—all victims being sufficiently nasty to cause us to reserve outright condemnation—require no explanation. Eventually he persuades Starling to share a meal with him comprising the pre-frontal cortex, sautéed with shallots, of a particularly evil individual. They then become lovers, and depart for Buenos Aires. It might be the case that Harris, with Lecter, attempts to catch the reader between feelings of abomination and awestruck reverence, and it is equally possible that he fails in both respects. As Martin Amis puts it, who could take seriously such an exercise in 'profound and virtuoso vulgarity' (*The War Against Cliché*, p. 241). Patricia Highsmith and Ira Levin have created figures who cause us to wonder about the boundaries between how human beings ought to behave and how they can, and in doing so they also make us doubt the quality of Harris's novels. Harris does not raise such questions. He suffocates them with an excess of the grandiloquent and the macabre.

The legal drama

The most elusive marginal sub-species of crime writing is the so-called legal drama, and curiously, the only crime novel classified unequivocally as a literary classic, *To Kill a Mockingbird*, belongs in this category. Since the *Newgate Calendar* the trial has featured in the various recipes for crime writing but few novels focus primarily upon the relationship between the accused, their advocate, the prosecution, and the machinery of the judicial system. Collins's *The Woman in White* reflects its author's early experience of legal cases as a student in Lincoln's Inn, with each of the narrators resembling witnesses whose testimonies often provide very different accounts of what actually occurred. In *The Law and the Lady* (1874) he examines legal procedure in more detail by having Valeria Brinton investigate accounts of the trial which delivered the verdict of 'not proved'—that is, neither guilt nor innocence could be absolutely proven—when her husband Eustace was tried for the murder of his first wife.

The first writer to build a career upon the stories of a practising lawyer and his various cases was the American Melville Davisson Post. His successful collection *Rudolph Mason: The Strange Schemes* (1896) tells of how the eponymous lawyer is an unashamed opportunist, making use of legal loopholes or even forging evidence to enable his clients to escape prosecution and punishment. In the 1930s Erle Stanley Gardner invented Perry Mason as a sanctimonious rejoinder to his predecessor.

Replicating his surname was the equivalent of throwing down a duellist's gauntlet. Perry Mason has earned himself a far more durable and honourable heritage, partly because he became the subject of a long-running television series starring Raymond Burr. Perry is as ruthless and cunning as Randolph but he manipulates procedure only to rescue the unjustly accused.

Perry Mason's British counterpart arrived a generation later with John Mortimer's Horace Rumpole. Rumpole's wryly comic ordeals at the Old Bailey began as plays for radio and television and were later rewritten as short stories. Virtually all mutations between the stage, screen, media, and print go in the other direction and Rumpole's reversal of convention tells us much about the nature of legal drama; specifically that it is an activity where theatre—involving a group of characters, a tense interaction between statements, denials, and challenges—is acted out before an audience. One of the best films ever made was adapted from a play and never went into prose form. *Twelve Angry Men*, which focuses exclusively on a jury debate in a murder trial, is driven by the electricity of dialogue and the pressures caused by the jurors' confinement in a single room.

Harper Lee's *To Kill a Mockingbird* (1960) is canonized in the US not only as a literary great but also as a key document in the history of the country and an exercise in moral and political enlightenment. No one graduates from High School without having read it. Atticus Finch defends Tom Robinson, a black man, against the accusation that he raped a white woman, Mayella Ewell. Within the twenty years prior to the novel's publication there had been several similar cases in which black defendants had been found guilty, executed by state authorities and on two occasions lynched and mutilated. The novel engaged with an unchallenged protocol: in the southern states a black accused of a crime against a white woman was guilty by default of race. But Lee's work was more than a polemic. We see it mainly from the perspective of 6-year-old Scout Finch, Atticus's daughter, who senses the gravity of her father's undertaking but does not properly understand his job or the grotesque nature of the town in which she lives. Robinson is found guilty, as we expect, and he is shot trying to escape. But we have to ask ourselves: is he innocent by virtue of counter-racism? Or might he have committed the crime?

A Time to Kill (1989) was John Grisham's first novel and he intended us to read it as a modern version of Lee's classic. Carl Lee Hailey's (note the 'Lee') 10-year-old daughter is raped by two white racists and Carl suspects that the predominantly white jury will be lenient. He shoots the accused dead and is defended against a murder charge by attorney Jake Brigance, assisted by liberal northern states volunteer Ellen Roark, his friend and drinking partner, the sleazy divorce advocate Harry Rex Vonner, and the disbarred, alcoholic gentleman attorney Lucien Wilbanks. Grisham's message seems to be that the liberal, enlightened consensus will prevail and Hailey is indeed found not guilty.

These novels have two significant factors in common, a white jury drawn from a still conservative Southern county and a black defendant. Perhaps, as Grisham suggests, the South has changed, but should we treat these books as indices to social transition or as literary works that reflect a far more complex gallery of private impulses and passions?

Chapter 7
Can crime fiction be taken seriously?

High and low culture

Despite Conan Doyle's ironic comment (via Watson, Figure 5), the answer to the question posed by the title of this chapter is yes. As we have seen, there are crime novelists whose work engages with profound social, moral, and existential issues, and crime writing can claim among its practitioners some of the finest literary stylists. But this question raises another. Even if some crime fiction demands our respect, why is it as a whole still treated as a sub-species of mainstream literature?

In the review columns of newspapers and magazines, crime writing is apportioned a separate place for critical scrutiny, usually half a page, implying that it merits different evaluative criteria from the 'literary' novel. This form of genre-apartheid resurfaces in the inclinations of established authors to take on pseudonyms when shifting their talents towards crime. C. Day Lewis becomes Nicholas Blake, Julian Barnes is Dan Kavanagh, and John Banville appears as Benjamin Black. This is not a genuine strategy of self-concealment—each is aware that their true identity will eventually be disclosed—but rather a mannerism, much in the same way that social mores once taught us to 'dress down' for certain occasions. Even among those writers who dedicate themselves exclusively to crime writing, the adoption of

5. Contemporary print of Sherlock Holmes. 'I had no idea that such individuals exist outside of stories.' (Dr Watson, in *A Study in Scarlet*, on his fellow fictional creation, Sherlock Holmes)

pseudonyms is extraordinarily frequent. It is almost as if the nature of a subgenre so capricious and contrived demands a collateral gesture of pretence on the part of its author.

Few would deny that crime writing is different from other forms of fiction yet does its distinctness automatically qualify it as culturally and aesthetically inferior?

The first attempt to classify crime fiction as a significant intellectual undertaking was Marjorie Nicolson's 'The Professor and the Detective' (1929). Nicolson, an academic, bases her argument on the observation, which we must accept on trust, that a considerable number of her peers in the academy, the arts and sciences, are avid fans of detective novels. She asks the question of why this should be, much in the manner of someone who wonders why priests visit brothels, and concludes that this form of writing provides refuge from the ongoing modernist fashion for instability and anarchy. Crime fiction focuses upon the use of reason, by the detective and the reader, and as such 'it is an escape not from life but from literature', or at least the kind of literature that employs devices such as 'stream of consciousness'...to engulf us in its Lethean monotony'. Nicolson's piece, while poised and high-minded in its manner, is extraordinarily patronizing. It grants crime writing a kind of status by association—comparing it with works by Joyce, for example—while at the same time treating it as a source of effortless relaxation. Despite their apparent differences Nicolson has much in common with Edmund Wilson who in his famous 1945 article 'Who Cares Who Killed Roger Ackroyd?' stated that 'with so many fine books to read...there is no need to bore ourselves with this rubbish'. Wilson treats crime fiction as low-cultural idleness and Nicolson regards it as a kind of reassuring crossword puzzle for those unsettled by intellectual radicalism. She indulges it and he does not, but their perception of it as a subsidiary to serious writing is shared.

Thirty years later when the academic branch of literary criticism was becoming less concerned with literature per se than with its potential as a laboratory for theories on language, politics, gender, etc., crime fiction began to be treated as one among many 'discourses', the theoreticians of structuralism and post-structuralism having dispensed with the illusion that highbrow and popular culture differ in terms of quality.

Typically, Stefano Tani (1982) proposed that detective fiction is 'a reassuringly 'low' genre which is supposed to please the expectations of the reader', which might easily be misinterpreted as a reiteration of Nicolson and Wilson's view of it as intellectually undemanding and aesthetically downmarket. But Tani has renounced evaluative judgement as an approach to literature or anything else. He encloses 'low' in inverted commas because in his view notions of low, high, or middlebrow culture are delusional. Ed McBain's work no more deserves the classification as insubstantial, disposable reading than Proust's ranking as the epitome of great literary art; they simply occupy different branches of the same discourse.

The classic example of what happens when literary theory encounters detective fiction began with a 'seminar', later published as an article, by the psychoanalytical theorist Jacques Lacan on Poe's 'The Purloined Letter'. Lacan argued that the content of the letter is insignificant and that it exemplifies the notion of language and truth first promoted by Ferdinand de Saussure: the letter, like the signifier, exists only in relation to the structure of symbols which ensures that its meaning will ultimately be transient and displaced. Jacques Derrida, founder of the linguistic-philosophical school of deconstruction, responded that the letter lacks meaning only because Lacan caused the 'lack' to become its meaning, while blinding himself to its true significance: that the letter symbolizes castration, of the King by the Queen. Barbara Johnson intervened to suggest that the letter belongs all the time to the Queen, as a substitute for a phallus. The debate continued, and served as a magnet for theoreticians keen to advertise their own ideas on language, truth, and identity, and it is instructive, though not because of what its participants tell us about Poe or by implication about the subgenre he is deemed to have founded. Lacan and Derrida were not drawn to Poe because they were interested in detective fiction. The latter was a convenient cultural pretext for their more profound investigative agenda.

Forms of compromise

A far more engaging account of the significance of crime fiction comes from an indisputably high-cultural writer. In 'The Guilty Vicarage' (1948) W. H. Auden seems to be following a line similar to that taken by Nicolson but rather than adopt a clinical academic mode he is frank regarding his addiction to the genre and troubled by the different ways in which he has come to account for the various levels on which he responds to it, ranging from guilt to aesthetic appreciation. He feels that detective stories are the least worthy of praise because in most cases the reader identifies with the investigator and joins him or her in an attempt to restore order to society. This, in Auden's view, is not only a misuse of literary writing but a means of denying the genuine attractions of crime writing. Also, we enjoy the ghoulish thrill of witnessing the apprehension, even the punishment, of the perpetrator but the structure of the detective narrative enables us to pretend that our interest is more virtuous. Auden contends that we should not deny the unwholesome element of our taste, but rather give greater recognition to the kind of crime fiction which does not easily enable us to do so. He has in mind the kind of novel in which we are invited, sometimes obliged, to share the outlook and emotional preoccupations of killers. He refers to Dostoevsky's *Crime and Punishment* but concedes that Chandler and Hammett could be included in the same category.

Julian Symons in *Bloody Murder* came up with a formula for evaluating crime writing as literature that is superior to anything offered in academic studies. Symons concedes that Auden is shrewd and honest but finds fault with his division of the genre into two sub-categories, detective fiction and the crime novel, not because they are different—he accepts that they are—but because Auden and others automatically allocate a potential for artistic quality to the latter while denying it to the former. He compares them with Restoration comedy and Jacobean drama: 'nobody condemns Restoration comedy outright because it lacks the profundity of Jacobean drama' (p. 27). There are, he avers, 'gradations' within each: some Restoration dramatists outrank a considerable number of their Jacobean counterparts in terms of stylistic acuity, and similarly there are writers of detective novels that transcend the escapist 'puzzle' classification of their mode by attaining levels of excellence in dialogue and characterization that match anything in mainstream fiction.

He welcomes what he calls the 'double standard', 'so that one can say first of all that the characteristic detective story has almost no literary merit, and second that it may still be an ingenious, cunningly deceptive, and finely constructed piece of work' (p. 28). Equally, we should not automatically assume that a novel that follows *Crime and Punishment* in eschewing the formulaic structure of a puzzle will match the masterful style of Dostoevsky in its execution.

Symons points out that the boundaries between crime writing and serious literature can often be blurred but in doing so he reinforces the case that such boundaries endure. So should we simply accept that crime fiction is by its nature largely inferior to the mainstream novel?

In chapter five of Symons's crime novel *A Sort of Virtue* (1996) we encounter an engaging description of the Pitcombes, a couple whose home in Belgravia is a magnet for left-liberal writers, media figures, and politicians. The Pitcombes themselves are green-movement affiliates and their hoard of provisions reflects their puritanical inclinations.

There was wine, of course, although orange juice and a drink which blended the pressings from eight vegetables were prominently displayed. And there was finger food, little pieces of cheese, meat and some fishy mixture, wrapped up in fragments to crumble in the hand before they could reach the mouth, and small cups of decaffeinated coffee. No spirits were served.

The passage provides a wry overture to our encounter with the guests, including figures who, we know, feel nothing more than indulgent contempt for the Pitcombes: particularly the noxiously ambitious MP, Bernard Bannock, and Donald Calendar, influential tabloid press baron, whose media empire was built on his successes in mid-range pornography. One can dip into the novel at random and come upon lengthy episodes such as this which equal anything from a sharply satirical, realist treatment of British society and politics of the mid-1990s. The difference is that while we savour Symons's clever unpicking of moral and political hypocrisies, we are also aware of something else, as if we are reading two novels simultaneously. Bannock is odious as an individual and a public figure but our interest in him as a fictionalized embodiment of political dissimulation is distracted by his role as murder victim. Symons's book presents us with a shrewd portrait of Britain in the 1990s but it also holds our attention as a murder-mystery. The line between the two generic sub-species is not clearly drawn, but does Symons's exercise in hybridization mean that we should classify him as inferior to classic realists?

In *City of Glass* (1988) the book's author, Paul Auster, enters the novel and comments on what the notion of 'crime' does to the reader. We become like a detective, alert to matters that might seem otherwise inconsequential, aware that we are reading two novels at the same time. We divide our attention between our sense of characters as variations upon the real world and their function as a repository of clues to matters such as motive, circumstantial evidence and ultimately, in the case of classic detective fiction—who committed the crime? But, Auster suggests, how different is this from what happens in 'literary' novels? In the latter too we are constantly gathering evidence, attempting to make sense of patently unreal creations—by definition, puzzles—and close the gap between what we think we know and what the next page will tell us.

Auster is far more self-consciously avant-garde in his manner than Symons but both deliberately raise questions about the difference between crime fiction and its high cultural counterpart, and in doing so both writers cause us to think again about our evaluative prejudices.

References

Chapter 1: Origins

Stephen Knight, *Form and Ideology in Crime Fiction* (London: Macmillan, 1980).

Michael Shepherd, *Sherlock Holmes and the Case of Dr Freud* (London: Tavistock Press, 1985).

Julian Symons, *Bloody Murder: From the Detective Story to the Crime Novel: A History* (2nd edn., Harmondsworth: Penguin, 1985).

Tzvetan Todorov, 'The Typology of Detective Fiction', in *The Poetics of Prose* (Oxford: Blackwell, 1977).

Chapter 2: The two ages: golden and hard-boiled

Raymond Chandler, 'The Simple Art of Murder', *The Atlantic Monthly*, December 1944 (repr. London: Vintage, 1988).

Father Ronald Knox, 'Detective Story Decalogue', in *The Art of the Mystery Story. A Collection of Critical Essays*, ed. H. Haycraft (New York: Carroll and Graf, 1992).

Review of *The Murder of Roger Ackroyd*, in *The Observer* (30 May 1926).

Review of *The Murder of Roger Ackroyd*, in *The Scotsman* (22 July 1926).

Dorothy L. Sayers, 'Introduction', *Great Short Stories of Detection, Mystery and Horror*, in *Modern Detective Fiction* (London: Gollancz, 1928).

Julian Symons, *Bloody Murder: From the Detective Story to the Crime Novel: A History* (2nd edn., Harmondsworth: Penguin, 1985).

Chapter 3: Transitions

P. D. James, *Talking About Detective Fiction* (London: Faber, 2012), p. 12.
The Cambridge Companion to Crime Fiction, ed. M. Priestman
    (Cambridge: Cambridge University Press, 2003).
Blackwell Companion to Crime Fiction, ed. C. J. Rzepka and
    L. Horsley (Oxford: Blackwell, 2010).
Joseph Wambaugh, *Hollywood Station* (New York: Little Brown,
    2006).

Chapter 4: International crime fiction

Fred Vargas (Frédérique Audoin-Rouzeau), Interview with the
    Guardian (18 January 2004).
The Wounded, Russian stories trans. G. Barnes and B. Lee (Hong
    Kong: Joint Publishing Company, 1979).

Chapter 5: Gender

Sue Grafton, *D is For Deadbeat* (New York: Henry Holt and Company,
    1987).
Sarah Paretsky, *Toxic Shock* (Harmondsworth: Penguin, 1988;
    published in the US as *Blood Shot*).

Chapter 6: Spy fiction, the thriller and legal drama

Martin Amis, *The War Against Cliché* (London: Jonathan Cape, 2001),
    p. 241.
John le Carré, interviewed in *Newsagent and Bookseller*, 30 November,
    1978, p. 22.
John le Carré, *The Spy Who Came In From the Cold* (New York:
    Coward–McCann, 1963).

Chapter 7: Can crime fiction be taken seriously?

Julian Symons, *Bloody Murder: From the Detective Story to the Crime
    Novel: A History* (1972; 2nd edn., Harmondsworth, Penguin, 1985).

Further reading

Chapter 1: Origins

A detailed, scholarly account of the pre-19th century origins of crime fiction in English is Ian Bell's *Literature and Crime in Augustan England* (London: Routledge, 1991). For a study of the broader contexts go to Douglas Hay et al. (eds.), *Albion's Fatal Tree. Crime and Society in Eighteenth Century England* (London: Allen Lane, 1976); and an intriguing study of the real-life subject of many early crime-based publications is offered by Gerald Howson in *It Takes A Thief: The Life and Times of Jonathan Wild* (London: Cresset Library, 1987). *A Counter-History of Crime Fiction* (Basingstoke: Palgrave-Macmillan, 2009) by Maurizio Ascari causes us to think again about the antecedents of crime writing, examining as it does the ways in which transgression and detection inform aspects of literature from the Classical period onwards.

For the period between the early 19th century and the ascendancy of Conan Doyle, begin with Keith Hollingsworth's *The Newgate Novel, 1830–1847* (Detroit: Wayne State University Press, 1963). On the Sensation Novel, Lyn Pykett's *The Sensation Novel from 'The Woman in White' to 'The Moonstone'* (Plymouth: Northcote House, 1994) is a concise accessible introduction; Winifred Hughes's *The Maniac in the Cellar: Sensation Novels of the 1860s* (Princeton: Princeton University Press, 1980) is more detailed and discursive.

On the later 19th century see: Clive Bloom et al. (eds.), *Nineteenth Century Suspense: From Poe to Conan Doyle* (Basingstoke: Macmillan,

1988), Clare Clarke's *Late Victorian Crime Fiction in the Shadows of Sherlock* (Basingstoke: Palgrave-Macmillan, 2014), and Sir Hugh Greene (ed.), *The Rivals of Sherlock Holmes: Early Detective Stories* (Harmondsworth: Penguin, 1972), a collection of crime stories published by popular, though now obscure, figures during the late 19th and early 20th centuries.

Chapter 2: The two ages: golden and hard-boiled

Colin Watson in *Snobbery with Violence: English Crime Stories and Their Audience* (London: Eyre and Spottiswoode, 1971) offers a wry account of the class-based nuances of British detective fiction between the First and Second World Wars. Le Roy L. Panek's *Watteau's Shepherds: The Detective Novel in Britain 1914–1940* (Bowling Green, OH: Popular Press, 1979) urges us to take the age of Christie more seriously while *The Puritan Pleasures of the Detective Story* (London: Gollancz, 1972) by Erik Routley is an engaging and unorthodox study of the genre from Conan Doyle to the late 1940s.

On the life and work of notable figures, Robert Barnard's *A Talent to Deceive: An Appreciation of Agatha Christie* (London: Collins, 1980) can be recommended, along with Janet Hitchman's *Such a Strange Lady: An Introduction to Dorothy L. Sayers* (London: New English Library, 1975) and S. T. Joshi's *John Dickson Carr: A Critical Study* (Bowling Green, OH: Popular Press, 1990).

David Geherin (*The American Private Eye: The Image in Fiction*, New York: F. Ungar, 1985) traces aspects of the Chandler generation back to Poe while William Marling's *The American Roman Noir: Hammett, Cain and Chandler* (Athens, GA: University of Georgia Press, 1998) offers a detailed study of narrative method and the social context of noir fiction. Geoffrey O'Brien in *Hardboiled America: Lurid Paperbacks and the Masters of Noir* (Cambridge, MA: Da Capo Press, 1997) is unusual and informative, concentrating on how hard-boiled writing became a minor branch of mainstream publishing and examining the cult status of book jacket illustrations, and the most detailed recent study of the social and political influences on the subgenre is Sean McCann's *Gumshoe America: Hard Boiled Crime Fiction and the Rise and Fall of New Deal Liberalism* (Durham, NC: Duke University Press, 2000). Biographers have been intrigued by the lives of men who created the most enduring American private detectives, notably:

Diane Johnson (*The Life of Dashiell Hammett*, New York: Random House, 1983); Roy Hoopes (*Cain: The Biography of James M. Cain*, Carbondale, IL: Southern Illinois University Press, 1987); Frank MacShane (*The Life of Raymond Chandler*, London: Jonathan Cape, 1976).

Chapter 3: Transitions

Several broad-ranging surveys of crime fiction include useful discussions of the changes that occurred in Britain and the US after World War II, particularly: Julian Symons's *Bloody Murder: From the Detective Story to the Crime Novel: A History* (1972; 2nd edn., Harmondsworth: Penguin, 1985), Stephen Knight's *Crime Fiction: 1800–2000. Detection, Death, Diversity* (New York: Palgrave-Macmillan, 2004), and Lee Horsley's *Twentieth Century Crime Fiction* (Oxford: Oxford University Press, 2005).

Bernard Benstock and Thomas F. Staley (*British Mystery and Thriller Writers since 1940*, Detroit: Gale, 1980) are good on crime writing in Britain between the 1940s and 80s. H. R. F. Keating edited *Crime Writers: Reflections on Crime Fiction* (London: BBC, 1978), which contains illuminating observations on their writing by the most important members of the post-war generation of British crime writers, and George N. Dove and Earl F. Bargainnier (eds.) produced a comparative study of British and US crime fiction during the same period (*Cops and Constables: American and British Fictional Policemen*, Bowling Green, OH: Popular Press, 1986).

Andrew Pepper (*The Contemporary American Crime Novel: Race, Ethnicity, Gender, Class* (Edinburgh: Edinburgh University Press, 2000), Ralph Willett (*The Naked City: Urban Crime Fiction in the USA*, Manchester: Manchester University Press, 1996), and Peter Messent (ed.), *Criminal Proceedings. The Contemporarary American Crime Novel* (London: Pluto Press, 1997) provide worthy guides to the various influences upon US crime fiction over the past three decades.

Chapter 4: International crime fiction

The best introduction to the history and nature of crime fiction beyond the British/American axis of the genre is not in printed form and has not, due to its author's illness, been updated since 2009. Nonetheless 'Landscapes of Crime' by the Dartmouth College Professor G. J. Demko can be easily accessed on the internet and offers enlightening insights into the development of crime writing in Continental Europe, Asia, and Latin America. The University of Wales Press (in alliance with University of Chicago Press) has recently launched a series of studies on International Crime Fiction, though so far all have focused on continental Europe: *Iberian Crime Fiction*, ed. Nancy Vosburg (Chicago: University of Chicago Press, 2011); *Italian Crime Fiction*, ed. Claire Gorrara (Cardiff: University of Wales Press, 2009); *Scandinavian Crime Fiction*, ed. Andrew Nestigan and Paula Arvas (Cardiff: University of Wales Press, 2011).

Of related interest is *Crime Fiction in the City: Capital Crimes*, ed. Lucy Andrew and Catherine Phelps (Cardiff: University of Wales Press, 2013), though the focus is once again upon European cities. *The Foreign in International Crime Fiction*, ed. Jean Anderson, Carolina Miranda, and Barbara Pezzotti (London: Bloomsbury, 2012) tends to focus on the theme of the transcultural, alien figure rather than on global crime fiction per se.

Chapter 5: Gender

Elizabeth Lindsay's *Great Women Mystery Writers* (Westport, CT: Greenwood Press, 2007) contains concise biographical and critical surveys of women crime writers from the 19th century onwards. For a study of the women writers who helped launch the crime fiction genre, some largely overlooked, go to *Women Writers and Detectives in Nineteenth Century Crime Fiction* by Lucy Sussex (Basingstoke: Palgrave-Macmillan, 2010). Since the 1980s there have been numerous studies of gender in crime fiction as a whole, and of women crime writers who make use of feminist methods and perspectives: Patricia Craig and Mary Cadogan, *The Lady Investigates: Women Detectives and Spies in Fiction* (London: Gollancz, 1981); Kathleen Gregory Klein, *The Woman Detective: Gender and Genre* (Urbana: University of Illinois Press, 1988); Sally R. Munt, *Murder by the Book? Feminism and the Crime Novel* (London: Routledge, 1994); Glenwood Irons (ed.), *Feminism in Women's Detective Fiction* (Toronto: Toronto University Press, 1995); Gill Plain, *Twentieth*

Century Crime Fiction: Gender, Sexuality and the Body (Edinburgh: Edinburgh University Press, 2001).

Chapter 6: Spy fiction, the thriller and legal drama

The most comprehensive accounts of thriller writing and related subgenres are Clive Bloom's (ed.) twin volumes, *Spy Thrillers: From Buchan to Le Carré* (Basingstoke: Macmillan, 1990) and *Twentieth Century Suspense: The Thriller Comes of Age* (Basingstoke: Macmillan, 1990). William V. Butler's *The Durable Desperadoes* (London: Macmillan, 1973) is a tongue-in-cheek survey of the mystery–spy thriller maverick from Robin Hood to James Bond, and David Stafford's *The Silent Game: The Real World of Imaginary Spies* (Athens, GA: University of Georgia Press, 2012) provides an illuminating account of how writers with actual experience of espionage, from Le Queux to le Carré, have produced the more notable spy novels of the past century. Jerry Palmer's *Thrillers. Genesis and Sructure of a Popular Genre* (London: Edward Arnold, 1978) is worth consultation.

More specialized academic studies include Ralph Harper, *The World of the Thriller* (Cleveland: Case Western Reserve University Press, 1969); Michael Denning, *Cover Stories: Narrative and Ideology in the British Spy Thriller* (London: Routledge, 1987); John G. Cawelti and Bruce A. Rosenberg, *The Spy Story* (Chicago: University of Chicago Press, 1987); Bruce Merry, *Anatomy of the Spy Thriller* (Dublin: Gill and Macmillan, 1977).

Chapter 7: Can crime fiction be taken seriously?

For books that tackle the unsteady relationship between crime fiction and high-brow literary culture begin with Julian Symons's *Bloody Murder*, an informed, balanced account of what the genre is and can do by one of its most astute practitioners. In the same vein H. R. F. Keating (ed.) in *Whodunit? A Guide to Crime Suspense and Crime Fiction* (London: Windward, 1982) offers a group of his fellow detective fiction writers the chance to reflect on the nature and significance of their trade. Martin Priestman in *Detective Fiction and Literature: The Figure on the Carpet* (Basingstoke: Macmillan, 1990) looks at crime writing from a cool academic perspective and judges it against its high cultural counterparts.

General reading

There are several general guides aimed primarily at an academic readership but made accessible enough for the general reader, notably: *The Oxford Companion to Crime and Mystery Writing*, ed. R. Herbert (Oxford: Oxford University Press, 2000); *The Cambridge Companion to Crime Fiction*, ed. M. Priestman (Cambridge: Cambridge University Press, 2003); *Crime Fiction* by John Scaggs (London: Routledge, 2005); *The Wiley Companion to Crime Fiction*, ed. C. J. Rzepka and L. Horsley (Oxford: Wiley–Blackwell, 2010).

For the reader who simply enjoys the genre the following can be recommended: P. D. James's *Talking About Detective Fiction* (London: Faber, 2012); Barry Forshaw's *The Rough Guide to Crime Fiction* (London: Rough Guide, 2007); Nick Rennison and Richard Shephard's *100 Must Read Crime Novels* (London: Bloomsbury, 2006).

Index